Desolation Pass

Alejandro del Pelado is a convicted murderer, sentenced to hang by the neck until dead. But at his execution things go horribly awry and he escapes to terrorize an unsuspecting town.

When a mysterious telegram draws Jim Hannigan and his lovely partner Angela 'Tootie' del Pelado into a twisted plot of kidnapping and revenge, the ex-manhunter begins to suspect an old enemy had come back to haunt them.

Within hours of their arrival in the former silver boomtown of Widow's Pass they find themselves at the mercy of a masked killer and his deadly cronies – two dandy hardcases and a vicious gypsy – who promise to make this case Hannigan's last.

Desolation Pass

Lance Howard

A Black Horse Western

ROBERT HALE · LONDON

ISBN 978-0-7090-8328-3

Robert Hale Limited
Clerkenwell House
Clerkenwell Green
London EC1R 0HT

www.halebooks.com

Typeset by
Derek Doyle & Associates, Shaw Heath
Printed and bound in Great Britain by
Antony Rowe Limited, Wiltshire

For Tannenbaum

CHAPTER ONE

November. . . .

It wasn't supposed to end this way. Hanging was for the weak, men too stupid to plan for every contingency, men too fragile to do what needed to be done, even if it meant murdering their own kin.

Darkness washed over Alejandro del Pelado's face as he walked the frost-hardened main street of Angel Pass, wrists bound behind his back. The chilled breeze sliced through his ragged circus-style shirt, but he barely felt it. A gunmetal dawn sky spat crystals of snow that stung his bearded face, yet he refused to flinch. His one good eye – the left covered by a patch – focused on the platform a hundred feet ahead, then shifted to the hooded figure standing upon it. The figure's hand rested on a lever that, when pulled, would release a trapdoor. A noose, frayed, blackened with mold, swayed, beckoning.

At the base of the gallows stood three men, members of the town council who had convicted him in a farce of a trial. Their faces and body language betrayed myriad emotions: annoyance at being dragged out into the cold at such an early hour, displeasure at the time it was taking to walk the prisoner from the jailhouse to the platform . . . and fear. Fear that somehow the man they'd come to watch die might somehow escape his fate and wreak terrible vengeance upon them.

He almost smiled.

To the left of the platform stood another man, one whom he vaguely recognized as the father of a boy he had kidnapped in another town, a boy whose body had been discovered on a lonely Colorado trail. Could he help it if the men to whom he'd sold that boy had been unable to deliver their property to whatever fate they intended for him? Was he responsible for what happened to those he sold into slavery after they left his hands?

The father certainly thought so. He had testified at the trial to that effect, and but for the marshal and deputy flanking him on either side that man would have saved the town a hanging and put a bullet straight through Alejandro's black heart. He could see the hate scrawled across the man's face.

But Marshal Wentworth and the council refused to allow that man the luxury of ending Alejandro del Pelado's life. In their infinite wisdom, they'd deemed this walk to the gallows and the contemplation of his crimes on this grey execution morning a more appropriate punishment.

A scene flashed before his mind, dragging him back to a day long ago, when he'd been a child. Men had ridden into the del Pelado ranch, a famous gunfighter and his partner, though Alejandro had not known that until just a few days ago when the marshal had delivered a newspaper recounting the circumstances of a man named James Deadwood's demise at the hand of one Jim Hannigan.

The name jarred him from the errant memory. Hannigan. So that sonofabitch had not only robbed him of a sister he'd searched years to find, but the satisfaction of delivering the vengeance he had dreamed on countless nights of doling out to his parents' killers as well. He wondered what Angela thought of that, why she hadn't been the one to put a bullet into the lowly bastard who destroyed their lives. Details. Details he didn't know, would go to his death never learning. Details that piqued his curiosity yet at the same time unearthed more rage within him than any man was capable of enduring.

'Hannigan. . . .' he whispered, hate bleeding from the word.

'What's that, Vago?' Marshal Wentworth asked, the older man's face grim. His new snakeskin boots thudded on the hard-packed ground.

Vago: the alias he had used for years. It no longer seemed to fit him. It left nothing but bitterness on his tongue. It was the name of failure.

'Don't call me that,' he muttered, head lifting, his tangled dark hair falling unbridled over his forehead. The scar running from his forehead to his cheek seemed to wriggle, like some sort of white snake that sensed the doom waiting, now a mere seventy-five feet away.

'I don't give a damn what you want to be called.' The marshal prodded Alejandro forward with a sharp push to a shoulder. 'The sooner we're rid of you, the sooner this town can get back to normal, least as normal as it can after a monster like yourself's left his stain on it.'

'Monster, Wentworth?' Alejandro uttered a chopped laugh. 'I did those children a favor. I granted them the opportunity to be strong.'

The marshal's face darkened and he scratched at his mutton-chop whiskers. 'Reckon their folks don't see it that way. The only favor you'll do any of those kids is dancing your last at the end of that rope.' Wentworth ducked his chin toward the gallows. 'We found most of them, incidentally. Just got word last night.'

'You have a reason for telling me that?' Rage boiled within Alejandro's belly. He wanted to put a knife into the lawman, watch the life bleed out of him, spit on his writhing body.

Wentworth's smile carried a note of satisfaction. 'Just wanted to give you a bit of comfort before we stretched your neck.'

'Yet you call me the monster,' Alejandro whispered.

Wentworth shrugged. 'Don't mistake my delight at your passing as a lack of compassion, *Vago*.'

'Compassion?' He uttered a scoffing *hmmph*. 'I want no compassion from you. Compassion is for the weak.'

Wentworth frowned. 'Don't worry, you won't get any from me. My compassion extends solely to the parents whose children we didn't find. They'll likely spend the rest of their days suffering with the hell

10

you brought to their lives. My compassion also extends to that sister of yours. From what Hannigan told me she's been through enough. You did nothing to ease her burden.'

Alejandro's face hardened. 'She's weak. She deserves whatever she gets.'

He stumbled then. His boot hooked a stone embedded in the hard ground as an odd feeling washed through his legs. Weakness? No, it couldn't be. He simply refused to allow that.

The deputy at his side grabbed his arm, preventing him from falling. The man chuckled and shook him harder than needed. Alejandro gave him a vicious look that wiped the jovial expression off the man's face. Another weakling. Easily intimidated.

Fifty feet remained. The gallows loomed against the gray backdrop like some mythical beast of death. He could hear the creaking of its wood from the cold; it sounded like the cries of dying children. He quickly forced the thought away. He didn't care for the fluttery sensation it caused in his belly. It reminded him too much of fear.

Twenty-five feet to go. It wasn't supposed to end this way, he told himself again. He was supposed to have been a farmer, like his father, with a family and a simple, satisfying life. Instead he was a man adrift in a sea of blood and fury.

He spat then, let out an enraged sound at his weak thoughts.

'Shut the hell up, Vago!' Marshal Wentworth poked him hard in the ribs. He glared at the lawman, then looked ahead again.

Where was she? Alejandro wondered. Angela should have been here to watch him hang. Why hadn't she come? At least to gloat? But Angela didn't gloat, did she? She had grown too weak, too kind. It disgusted him. He would have gladly watched her die had the situation been reversed.

They reached the stairs and he looked up at the hooded figure, who didn't move. His gaze traveled to the rope again, which still swayed. More snow crystals spat from the unsympathetic sky and snipped at his face.

A thought rose unbidden in his mind: He didn't want to die. No matter how many times he had claimed not to fear death, he discovered much to his dismay and disgust that when facing it he might have feared it indeed.

'I'm weak,' he said under his breath, the words laced with revulsion. 'How can that be?' How could the years of hell he'd experienced after leaving his uncle's home not have forged a man of iron will and soulless constitution? He was pathetic, no better than those children he'd sold, no better than. . . .

His sister.

'Damn you, Hannigan!' he shouted, his control snapping. He wrenched himself around, tried to run.

Wentworth and the deputy grabbed him and he struggled like a wretched frightened animal. He kicked at them, bit at their groping hands. The marshal hammered a fist against Alejandro's forehead, ending his resistance. His legs threatened to desert him; only their supporting grip prevented him from collapsing to his knees.

'Damn, I think the sonofabitch is gonna bawl,' the deputy said, pulling Alejandro onto the first step.

'Up!' Wentworth ordered.

Alejandro felt himself half-comply, half be yanked up the steps to the platform.

What the hell was wrong with him? He felt like that lost child who'd stumbled into the outlaw camp shortly after he'd run away from his uncle's home. But what those men had done to him had only made him stronger . . . stronger. . . .

'Strong!' he shouted. 'I am strong!'

The marshal slapped him full across the face and Alejandro's head rocked. 'I said shut the hell up, Vago. Go out like a man, for chrissake.'

Alejandro went silent, the reality of the situation overwhelming him. For the barest of moments something rose within him that he might have labeled regret, a kind word for a sister he had lost years before, only to find a few short weeks ago. But the notion was fleeting, instantly despicable. He was what he was:

A monster.

They walked him to the dangling noose and turned him towards the father whose son had been found dead. The man peered up at him with a mixture of enraged hatred and maybe the expectancy of some explanation, some meager attempt at an apology for his crimes. The man would die waiting for that, Alejandro thought. No sympathy remained within him. Only contempt. He cast him a sly smile and the man's face reddened. His hand drifted to the gun at his hip, settled on the grip; but he didn't draw. That man wanted to watch him swing now, was eager with anticipation for it.

Wentworth placed the noose over Alejandro's head and yanked it tight. The fibers bit into his flesh. He drew a deep breath and steeled himself, eye narrowing with spite, defiance.

Marshal Wentworth looked at him, face grim. 'You got a prayer to say, Vago, now's the time to spit it out.'

'Go to hell, Wentworth,' he said, staring straight head.

Wentworth shook his head. 'Reckon you'll blaze the trail. . . .'

The marshal backed away, to the edge of the platform. The deputy did the same.

'May God have mercy on your soul,' Wentworth muttered, eyes pained. 'And mercy on those whose lives you darkened. . . .'

The marshal glanced at the hooded man and gave a slight nod.

The hangman's hand tightened on the lever, in preparation for yanking it back.

A shot thundered through the gray morning. The sound of it came so startling, so unexpected, that Wentworth jumped half a foot off the platform. The deputy started and Alejandro stiffened. The hangman's hand froze on the lever. An instant later he fell face first to the platform boards.

'What the goddamn hell—' Wentworth jerked from his surprise and his hand went for the gun at his hip.

Another shot followed and Alejandro could tell now that it came from a rooftop across the street.

Wentworth never drew his gun. A crimson orchid bloomed on his chest. He crumpled to the platform without a sound.

The deputy swung, also drawing a bead on the source of the gunfire. It did him no good. With the thunder of a third shot he flew backwards off the platform and crashed onto the hard-packed street. He spasmed, then lay still, a gaping hole over his heart.

Alejandro wasted no more time with shock. He tugged at the ropes binding his wrists, flesh tearing, blood running. He ignored the pain skewering his hands and forearms. Blood greased the ropes and he managed to pull a hand free. Bringing his hands to the front, he pried the noose loose and lifted it over his head.

The father who'd come to witness the hanging jerked from his shock and went for his gun. Alejandro dived for the body of the marshal, in nearly the same move grabbing the lawdog's Colt from its holster. He swung the piece towards the father just as the man got his own gun aimed. Two shots came concurrently. The father jumped backwards, lead punching through his sternum. He slammed into the ground on his back, lay unmoving.

Alejandro scrambled backward as lead plowed into the platform at his feet.

Another shot came from the nearby rooftop and the councilman who'd fired the shot at Alejandro flew backwards to the dirt.

Alejandro swung his Colt, triggered a shot. Lead shattered the face of the second councilman, killing

15

him instantly.

With a final blast, the third man pitched face forward to the street, terror and shock a death mask on his features.

The gray morning became eerily quiet. Blue smoke drifted from the gun in Alejandro's hand. He gazed about at the bodies, a ghost of a smile on his lips.

A shout snapped him from his thoughts, female, familiar:

'Go to the clearing, just outside the north end of town where you set up the carnival. Five minutes.'

As he rose to his feet from a crouch, he nodded. Jamming the marshal's Colt into his waistband, he scrambled down the stairs. A horse stood tethered to a hitch rail a dozen feet away, likely the dead father's mount. He ran to it, grabbed the reins, then jumped into the saddle. With a slap of his heels he sent the animal galloping forward, eager to put the town behind him before someone came to investigate the shots and saw the carnage.

As he drove the mount through the street a few doors flew open. It wouldn't take them long to organize a posse. Too many had cheered the day his death sentence was pronounced and he wasn't about to give them a second chance to stretch his neck.

Two minutes of riding found him at the clearing, which was now empty of the circus wagons and tents that had attracted crowds just a few weeks before. He wondered what had become of all his equipment, but going back to find it was no longer an option.

He reined up, gaze sweeping the area; he saw no

one. After dismounting, he drew the Colt again and waited.

Hoofbeats sounded from behind him and he spun to see a woman riding towards him, a rifle in one hand, reins wrapped about the other. Her dark curls bounced on her shoulders and her large breasts strained at a tan blouse. Glimpses of olive flesh showed from a slit in her riding-skirt.

She slowed to a halt, shoved the rifle into a saddle-boot and smiled. Her cheeks were rouged and her dark-brown eyes, hard and satisfied, narrowed.

She urged the horse closer to him, peered down.

'Madam Mystique . . . Carmella . . .' Alejandro shoved the Colt back into the waist of his trousers. 'I wondered what had happened to you.'

She spat, face darkening with anger. 'Hannigan and his whore happened to me. I spent a week in jail. But they had nothing to hold me on, so they had to let me go. I came looking for you.'

'You cut it close.' His voice sharpened. Strength filled him again. This woman had disappeared weeks ago, right before Angela had come to him for a job at his carnival. He knew she and Hannigan must have done something with Carmella, but didn't know what.

She shook her head, black curls bobbing. 'Couldn't be helped. They had you guarded so well I was forced to wait till they brought you out into the open.'

'We have to go. Now. Won't take long 'fore the town figures out what happened.'

'Some of the others, they're still in jail.'

17

Alejandro's face hardened. 'Leave them.'

'What?' Shock swept over her olive features. She clearly didn't like the idea, but he didn't give a damn.

'I said, leave them. Let them swing. We'll hire new blood.'

Alejandro del Pelado spun, then mounted his horse. Turning his head back to her, he gave her a dark smile before heeling the animal into a gallop. The shock on her face pleased him. He knew it would give him more power over her, more control. She would see him as the ruthless sonofabitch he wanted to be seen as. And that was good thing, indeed.

CHAPTER TWO

Six months later. . . .

Jim Hannigan knew the summons to Widow's Pass,
Colorado, was a fake, but he had come anyway. The
message had aroused his manhunter's curiosity.
Someone had gone to a wagonload of trouble to lure
him to this town and he intended to give them their
money's worth. Was it a trap? He would have bet on
it. But if it was he preferred walking into it of his own
free will instead of chancing a bullet he didn't see
coming. This way allowed him to maintain a certain
amount of control over the situation and take
precautions.

The telegram had arrived a week ago, at his
Denver office. Brief in detail, it offered a simple
proposition: find the missing daughter of one
Majenta de la Vaga, a woman of means who lived in
Widow's Pass. The missive had promised a great deal
of money, provided the details of the meeting. In
itself, that wasn't particularly suspicious. But accord-
ing to Hannigan's preliminary research, no woman
named Majenta de la Vaga existed, rich or otherwise.

The name had not checked out through any of his sources, which, Hannigan wagered, probably meant it was concocted. That had set his manhunter's sixth sense to buzzing.

But if indeed it proved to be a trap – and certainly plenty of hardcases had a bullet with Hannigan's name on it – why go to so much trouble? Why not simply ambush him?

An answer rose unbidden: Because whoever had called him here wanted more than simply to kill him. Whoever this mysterious Magenta de la Vaga turned out to be, she – if it were actually a woman – wanted a reckoning. She knew Hannigan would peg the message for a set-up and come to investigate. Someone knew his methods and his nature and was endeavoring to use it to their advantage.

That meant that someone was likely known to him in some way, someone from his past.

At this junction, he might be making leaps in logic, he told himself. But as many times as he came up with alternative reasons for the subterfuge – someone of high stature wishing to remain anonymous until the details of the transaction were secure, someone fearful for her own life who chose to remain hidden until the very last minute – he could not shake the notion that death awaited him in this town.

That's why he hadn't come alone.

A ghost of a smile brushed his lips as he stepped onto the boardwalk in front of the Regency Hotel. He doubted he could have gotten out of his Denver office without a certain Miss Angela del Pelado following him anyway.

The mid-spring night was warm. A damp breeze made hanging signs creak, and gaslights fluttered. Puddles from the previous night's rain glimmered with captured light on the hard-packed, wide main street. Wisps of steam drifted up like lost phantoms. A handful of folks sauntered along the boardwalks, though the sun had retreated into the distant mountains hours earlier. In the distance the mournful wailing of a train haunted the night.

Widow's Pass – so named because of a number of unfortunate mining accidents early in its founding – was again a thriving town, expanding in bounds, after years of dwindling population and interest after its lifeblood, silver, had trickled out. Its founder, silver baron Thaddeus Cambridge, despondent over the loss of his fortune after mines and market went bust, had shot himself in the head in the drawing room of his mansion. The mansion, abandoned, still existed north of town; Hannigan had seen its dark hulk, in sad disrepair, on his ride in.

But like a Sterling phoenix, the town had risen from the ashes after track had been laid at its northernmost end. With the railroad came prosperity and the resultant mushrooming of businesses, both legitimate and sporting.

The Regency was a better class of hotel than Hannigan usually frequented when on cases. As he stepped into the lobby, boots making an unnaturally loud slap on the high-polished, marble-tiled floor, he nearly let out a whistle. Not only had someone gone to a lot of trouble to bring him here but they had arranged the meeting in a place he would not have figured for an ambush. 10:30, REGENCY HOTEL, the telegram had said; THE 13TH, ROOM 10.

His gaze roved, taking in the luxury of the place. The lobby held a gaslit crystal chandelier, mahogany furniture of rich Victorian styling, imported from the East. An ornate oval carpet lay beneath the chandelier, from the Orient, he reckoned.

A fancy-suited clerk who stood behind a counter of rich dark wood gazed at him. A look of disdain crossed his face. He had obviously made a snap judgment based on Hannigan's attire: blue bib shirt, battered Stetson, brown trousers and worn boots, the one on the right with a sheath holding a Bowie. Likely the gun at his hip didn't help matters, since he noticed the handful of men lounging about the lobby weren't heeled.

Music and singing drifted from the hotel restaurant to his left. A deep contralto voice sang, 'I'll Take You Home Again, Kathleen.'

'Room ten?' he asked the clerk, when he reached the counter. The clerk's gaze dropped, focusing on the black-leather register with gilt lettering that rested on the polished countertop.

'We don't cater to your type here, sir.' The clerk didn't bother to look up as he said it, apparently hoping Hannigan would simply walk away, but afraid he wouldn't.

Hannigan suppressed a prickle of irritation. His hazel eyes narrowed. 'Wasn't asking for a room for myself. I'm supposed to meet someone here.'

'Yes?' The man looked up with a raised eyebrow. 'I

assure you *that* type of woman does not frequent this establishment, sir.'

Hannigan surveyed the man. He was a slight fella, cocky of carriage, but a worried look danced in his mouse-colored eyes. While the man's attitude was certainly trying Hannigan's nerves, the manhunter noticed something else behind his demeanor – he was purposely trying to delay him. As if confirming that thought, the clerk shifted slightly and Hannigan figured he knew why.

Hannigan grabbed a handful of the fellow's vest and hauled him over the counter. The clerk uttered a squawk but offered no resistance. The manhunter hurled him into a scarlet wing-backed chair that sat beside the counter. He then walked around to the back of the counter and studied the floor where the clerk had been standing. A small button caught his attention. He looked back to the startled clerk.

'Reckon I already know the answer, but what's the button for?'

The man licked his lips, fiddled with his watch chain, thin hand trembling. 'It's . . . it's a courtesy for our higher-paying customers, the ones who book room 10. It rings in the room to inform them when their guests have arrived.'

Hannigan nodded, his suspicion confirmed. 'Someone paid you to notify them when I came in.' It wasn't a question and from the way the man in the chair squirmed it didn't need an answer.

'How'd you recognize me?' Hannigan came back around the counter and stood in front of the man. Looking him over carefully, he decided the clerk posed no threat. He saw no suspicious bulges that indicated weapons beneath his suit coat and the fellow didn't appear to have the backbone to try to fight his way out of his predicament.

'Your ... your picture was in the paper a few months back; someone showed it to me.'

'Someone?'

The man didn't answer, but his face went a shade whiter. Hannigan leaned over the chair, grabbed both arms and shoved his face close the other man's.

'I asked you a goddamn question. . . .'

The clerk tried to press himself deeper into the chair. 'A . . . a woman. Mexican girl. Said you were a friend of hers and she wanted to surprise you. Said you were a longtime *close* friend. I didn't like the idea of your type coming in here but she paid me . . . a lot.'

Hannigan gave the man a slight smile. 'You do realize if I don't come back from my meeting with her you won't live long enough to spend the money?'

'W-what do you mean?'

'If you saw my picture you know who I am and what I do. I reckon even a dim fella such as yourself can connect the dots from there.'

The man appeared too frightened to take Hannigan's slight with any indignation. 'S-she lured you here . . . paid me to tell her when you arrived.'

Hannigan smiled again, patted the man's cheek hard a couple times. 'See, you got some smarts after all. Reckon I don't have to suggest you take the rest of the night off and not come back to work for a spell.'

The man gave a jackrabbit nod.

Hannigan straightened. 'Now, room ten?'

'Up the stairs, down the hall. . . .'

'Much obliged.' Hannigan tipped a finger to his hat, then headed for the stairs. He noticed the folks in the lobby eyeing him with looks of disgust and dismay after witnessing his display with the clerk, but none seemed inclined to make a threatening move. Nevertheless, he kept an eye on them as he climbed the stairs.

Barter Clancy scurried into the back room as soon as Jim Hannigan reached the top of the stairs. Anger washed away some of the fear now that that – that *rascal* had left. How utterly oafish that man was! Barter simply could not believe men still acted in such a vulgar manner, but he should have known better than to come to this, this mud-hole of a town from the more genteel society of Boston. Earn more money, Hilda had told him. See the untamed wilderness and ever-changing West, she had blathered. He would certainly have a discussion with her when he arrived home tonight! That wife of his was going to answer for uprooting him from fine society and persuading – no, *demanding* he relocate to this utterly uncivilized, vermin-infested hole.

But first he had to deal with the matter of his own safety. Whatever lowlife that man Hannigan might be, he had a point. Someone had made a dupe of Barter Clancy and would never let him live to spend the cash he had been promised, and not yet been paid, he might add. If Hilda had been in error forcing him to come West, then he could lay claim to a whopper of a blunder in accepting that proposition from that Mexican woman. But she'd been so . . . *convincing*. His face reddened when he thought of the ways she had persuaded him to take her proposition; he prayed Hilda never discovered that little imbroglio or that whoever wanted to know about Hannigan's arrival wasn't going to be the only person looking to settle his bill.

A low-turned light burned on the wall in the back room. Shadows clotted in the corners. As he shut the door, he nearly jumped out of his Hildeburger leather shoes.

Someone stood behind the door, waiting. Barter uttered a chopped bleat. His nerves were strung so tight a mouse would have sent him hopping onto a chair.

'I believe we have business to settle?' the man said, his face partly in shadow. He was big, with an eyepatch and a salted beard, dressed in a loose shirt, brown pants and high circus-type boots.

'W-who are you?' Barter managed to force out, sweat springing out on his forehead.

The bearded man smiled. It wasn't a pleasant smile, more like a snake about to swallow a mouse. 'I am an associate of the woman who hired you. I've come to settle up.'

'That's quite all right, sir, no payment necessary, I assure you—'

Barter's words ended in a liquidy gurgle as the man's hand came from behind his back and buried a knife in Barter's bread basket.

When Hannigan reached the top of the stairs he paused, gaze taking in the long hallway before him. Gaslights glimmered on walls covered in rich foil papering. A thick carpet ran the length. Credenzas and tied velvet drapes were spaced at even intervals. Numerous doors showed, all exhibiting a gilt number.

Two men stood in the hall, each lounging against the wall to either side of the door to Room 10. Each man was smallish, holding a cigarette in tapered fingers that might have belonged to a woman. Each had fragile, almost dainty features that never would have pegged them as hardcases or criminals of any sort. They wore odd clothing: loose billowy shirts and snug trousers with high boots that reminded Hannigan of the circus performers he'd encountered on a case last year. The two peered in his direction, smiled in unison, expressions that were neither inviting nor threatening, simply . . . mechanical, practiced.

Neither appeared heeled, but whoever had called him here had been forewarned by the clerk that he was on his way up, so their presence was too coincidental for his taste.

He walked towards them, rangy frame relaxing, ready to draw should one or both of the men pull a concealed weapon. The closer he got to them the more feminine they looked, though he was positive neither was a woman in disguise. Each dropped his cigarette onto the carpet, ground it out with a boot-toe.

'Gents. . . .' he said as he approached the door between them.

'Mr Hannigan. . . .' they said in unison, ending any doubt as to their connection to whoever had sent for him.

'You know me?' He kept his gaze on both men.

'Why, of course,' they both said.

'How?' he asked.

'Mr Rory's a big fan of yours,' the one to his left said, with a peculiar smile. 'Sometimes it even makes me jealous.'

'Mr Ryan speaks the truth, my dear man,' the other said, showing the same peculiar grin. 'You're certainly more handsome in person than in your picture. It's such a shame what the worms will do to your face—'

Mr Rory moved then, faster than anyone Hannigan had encountered in quite a spell. The little man slammed into Hannigan's side with surprising strength, hurling the manhunter back against the opposite wall.

Hannigan got no time to reflect on how such a small fellow could exhibit such strength because Mr Ryan, the second man, was on him like a writhing little snake. The man's limbs seemed made out of leather and elastic. He had a leg wrapped around Hannigan's calf and an arm crooked about the manhunter's right elbow, preventing him from getting to his gun. With his free hand, Mr Ryan tapped a stuttering series of blows into Hannigan's jaw that hurt like hell and carried more power than he would have thought possible in such close quarters.

28

Hannigan endeavored to dislodge the man, but that only seemed to tighten the fellow's grip.

Mr Rory leapt to his partner's aid. He kicked at Hannigan's free shin, grabbed at the manhunter's hair, after knocking the hat from his head, pulled hard. Mr Ryan tried to scratch out Hannigan's eyes but the manhunter jerked his head away – right into Mr Rory's pistoning fist.

'Christ!' Hannigan blurted, the blow stinging like a nest of hornets. He exploded from the wall, hurling Mr Rory away in the same move. It took every ounce of strength he had but he managed to disentangle himself from the little man and fling him into his partner.

Both attackers wasted no time being stunned. Quickly regaining their balance, they charged him, coming in low.

Hannigan swung an uppercut that practically lifted Mr Rory off the floor. He may have been strong for his size but he didn't carry much weight. The little hardcase hit the carpet on his ass, went heels over head backward.

Hannigan whirled, jerking up an arm as Mr Ryan jabbed a fist.

The jab nailed Hannigan's forearm, stung like hell. For a moment he thought his bone might have been fractured, but realized that Mr Ryan had purposely struck a bundle of nerves. The hardcase knew where to hit and where to hurt and half of Hannigan's arm went suddenly numb. He shook it, trying to get the feeling back.

At the same time the manhunter glided back,

giving himself room to maneuver. Pivoting, he snapped his leg up in a sidekick that took the now charging Mr Ryan in the chest with a hollow thud. The little hardcase bounced back like a kicked ball, hit the carpet and rolled like an acrobat.

Mr Rory slammed into Hannigan's back, throwing the manhunter forward. He rebounded face first from the wall, tried to whirl before his attacker could do any more damage.

Mr Rory's fist slammed into Hannigan's jaw; lights exploded before his eyes. Just as his vision cleared a second fist ricocheted off his temple.

Hannigan had all he could do to remain on his feet. His legs wanted to go in different directions and the hallway jumped back and forth before his eyes.

He shook his head, clearing his senses to see Mr Rory's grinning features looming before him.

'Oh, yes, so handsome, indeed.' Mr Rory jabbed another punch.

Hannigan snapped his head sideways on instinct. Mr Rory's punch missed and the manhunter countered with a fist straight down the pike. With the sound of a gunshot knuckles crashed into Mr Rory's jaw, which seemed to change shape. The little hardcase skipped backward and landed flat on his back, staring up at the hallway ceiling, dazed.

Mr Ryan grabbed Hannigan from behind. The manhunter twisted his hip and hurled the little hardcase over it the moment he felt the man's touch. Mr Ryan slammed into the floor with an exaggerated thump.

Hannigan watched both as they struggled to get

up. His breath beat out; sweat soaked his shirt and face. Every muscle burned and felt trembly.

With the back of his hand, he wiped a trickle of blood from his lip. 'Now, let's find out who the hell you're working for—'

Something crashed into the back of his head. His knees buckled, then blackness swept across his vision.

Madam Mystique stood over the unconscious form of Jim Hannigan, a pistol in her hand, a satisfied expression on her full lips. She hoped she hadn't killed him, hitting him so hard, but she had needed to make damn certain he stayed down. Of course, if she *had* killed him, Alejandro would likely kill her. His orders about keeping the manhunter amongst the living had been specific. Revenge on a dead man wasn't worth much, and neither would her life be if she had screwed up.

She shrugged, then eyed the two Nancy hardcases as they gained their feet. Mr Rory wiped blood from his mouth and Mr Ryan spat out a tooth.

'You two are goddamn near worthless,' she said, aiming the gun with which she had clocked Hannigan at them. She half-considered shooting them, but she needed someone to lug the body down the stairs.

'He was stronger than we thought,' Mr Ryan said, looking down at Hannigan, then giving him a vicious kick in the side.

'But handsome,' Mr Rory said. 'So very handsome.'

Madam Mystique laughed. 'He won't be after that train gets done with him. Pick him up and carry him down the back way. Alejandro will be waiting on us at the track by now.'

The hardcases nodded in unison, then bent to pick up Hannigan's unconscious form.

CHAPTER THREE

Angela 'Tootie' del Pelado blurted a word Jim Hannigan probably would have thought she didn't know. She reckoned he'd be shocked to discover half of what she'd picked up in the home where she'd spent most of her younger years. Whoever thought nuns didn't occasionally paint the air blue never resided with the Sisters of Holy Hellfire – the nickname she'd bestowed upon the strict order who had endeavored to scare righteousness into her.

She uttered the word because it appeared that skulking around in the dark behind hotels, no matter how careful a body tried to be, came with its share of hazards, stepping in horse-dung being one of them.

She hissed another curse and tried to scrape off the bottom of her high-laced shoe on a piece of board she found lying near the building opposite the back side of the hotel.

Scarcely any light from street-lanterns filtered into the alley in back of the Regency. While her eyes had adjusted somewhat, she could barely pick out the hotel's back door and the various obstacles: crates, refuse and horse flop littering the alley.

'Damn,' she muttered, after scraping the dung off her shoe. 'That smell's going to follow me around for a week.'

A sound reached her ears, distracting her from the odor. She listened intently. Sounds drifted in from the street: a coach clattering along, the muffled voices of passers-by, the clopping of hoofs. But those sounds hadn't caught her attention. Another noise had; the rattle of a doorknob being turned.

Eyes narrowing, she stared towards the hotel's back door. She crouched, gathering her skirt about her knees, waiting. Her hand eased to the derringer tucked in her skirt pocket. Her breath caught; her heart stepped up a beat.

Hannigan had been right to move her into place behind the hostelry, though she hadn't liked the idea of him walking into a possible trap alone one damn bit. He took too many chances, the way she saw it, and whoever had sent him that telegram had known that fact.

She hoped the door's opening furtively didn't mean something had happened to him.

A bolt of panic sizzled through her mind: what if he had been wounded, killed?

No, she refused to let herself think that. But if he came out of this in one piece she just might have to kill him herself for causing her so much worry.

The door creaked open all the way and she spotted a man backing through. He appeared to be carrying something. She straightened, tried to maneuver closer by edging along a stack of empty crates.

Her foot hit something in the dark, this time without the unyielding and odorous qualities of horse dung. A board. The board slid forward, struck a crate and made a sound loud enough to carry throughout the alleyway.

She froze, heart thudding in her throat. When the man coming through the door paused, her hand tensed on the derringer.

A heartbeat. Two. The man started backing out again and she let out the breath she'd been holding. She knew he had heard the sound but likely had passed it off as some animal scurrying from the alley.

She waited another moment, eyes narrowing again. The man wasn't carrying something, he was carrying some*one*. A second man held the front end of the form.

She didn't have to see a face to know who the form belonged to. She knew instinctively, like a mother knows her child is hurt, that it was Jim Hannigan. With the knowledge panic overrode her common sense.

She started forward. If they had hurt him—

Someone slammed into her, whirled her around, then hurled her against the brick wall of the building opposite the hotel. A knife jammed against her throat and a burning sensation followed, then a warm trickle down her neck.

A laugh sounded before her face and a burst of breath that smelled of tortilla and onion made her nostrils flinch. Despite the darkness Tootie recognized her attacker – Madam Mystique, the gypsy she waylaid months back when she and Hannigan

brought down her brother's child-snatching opera-
tion.

'I knew wherever Hannigan went you would
follow, *puta*. . . .' said the woman.

'I know you,' Tootie whispered, the blade pressing
into her throat making speech difficult. 'From Angel
Pass. . . .'

'*Sí, señorita.* You thought you were rid of Carmella,
did you not? But I never forget a debt.'

The men carrying the body from the hotel had
paused, each gazing toward the commotion.

Madam Mystique twisted her head toward them.
'You know where to take him. I'll be there shortly. I
have a score to settle with *la puta.*'

One of the men nodded and they hauled their
burden out the other end of the alley.

'Don't worry, *puta*, your man's alive – for the
moment. But he has a train to catch. You, on the
other hand, will not live long enough to mourn his
passing.'

Tootie acted. She saw no choice. She knew the
woman would slit her throat the moment she
finished speaking.

Tootie's fist snapped up, slammed into one of
Madam Mystique's ample breasts. In nearly the same
move, her other hand jack-knifed between the
gypsy's weapon hand and her own throat. The blade
jerked, bit into her palm, but that was better than her
throat.

Ignoring the pain, Tootie snapped her head sideways so the knife slashed past her hand; its tip ricocheted from the brick wall.

Doubling, Tootie swung her torso under the gypsy's arm. She jabbed a punch into the woman's ribs as she straightened again at Mystique's left side. The gypsy squawked, arced the knife in a backhand sweep at Tootie's face.

Tootie ducked, brought her knee up and snapped her shin into Madam Mystique's side. The gypsy staggered backward, shrieking curses and cleaving the air with the blade.

Bobbing and weaving, Tootie charged her, drilled a two-knuckled jab straight into the nerve center under the gypsy's knife arm.

Carmella bleated and the knife dropped from her suddenly nerveless fingers.

Tootie reckoned she had mere seconds to seize the advantage while the gypsy's arm was disabled. She remembered all too well her first near-loss encounter with the woman and preferred to end this fight as quickly as possible, so she could go after Hannigan before anything worse happened to him.

A fist slammed into her mouth just as she finished the thought. The gypsy, wasting no time in recovering, had struck with her good hand. The blow sent an explosion of stars cascading before Tootie's eyes and hurt like hell. Every one of her teeth ached and the coppery taste of blood soured her mouth.

The gypsy pounced like a mountain cat, battering her with a fist, kicking at her shins, biting at her face.

Tootie struggled to get her bearings. The gypsy grabbed a handful of hair and yanked.

'Dammit, not my hair, you stupid—' Tootie started, but got a forehead slammed into her mouth for her trouble.

Tootie staggered, the blow nearly knocking her from her feet. Her legs wobbled as weakness washed through her body. She'd lost focus only for an instant but the gypsy had taken full advantage of the lapse. What's more, the woman had gotten the use of her other arm back and was swinging it like a monkey winding the handle on a hurdy-gurdy.

Tootie's head bobbed left, then right, avoiding the brunt of the blows. One caught her on a shoulder and knocked her sideways.

The gypsy, unrelenting, swarmed over her. A panicky notion told Tootie she was going to lose if she didn't do something fast, and if she lost Jim Hannigan would die along with her.

The thought galvanized her. Adrenaline shot into her veins. She let out a yell and brought up both arms in a boxing defense.

The gypsy's blows bounced from her forearms. They hurt, but did little damage other than leave welts and bruises.

Tootie slid a foot forward, pivoted, then snapped up the other foot and buried it in the gypsy's middle.

Carmella doubled, gasping. Tootie launched an uppercut that collided with the gypsy's chin with a satisfying *clack*. Mystique staggered. Before the woman regained her balance Tootie fired three more punches that stung her knuckles.

The gypsy wobbled, pitching forward, legs nearly gone. Tootie whirled and delivered a high round-house kick that landed square against the gypsy's chin.

Carmella jolted upright, uttered a small squeal like a kicked kitten, then collapsed to her knees. Tootie hammered a punch into the gypsy's temple and Mystique fell face forward to the ground, groaning but unmoving. With a grunt, Tootie kicked her in the ribs for good measure.

Tootie, blouse torn, hair a tangle, lips swollen and blood running from her nose and mouth, gasped a breath, then sprinted from the alley. She couldn't waste time tying up the woman, not with Hannigan's life at stake.

A train to catch. That could only mean one thing: they had taken Hannigan to the railroad tracks north of town. As if in answer, a shrill whistle shrieked from the distance and she caught the muffled chugging of a locomotive rolling in from the east.

Worry energizing her, she ran to a horse tethered to a hitch rail and grabbed the reins. She launched herself into the saddle, swept the horse around and heeled it into a gallop.

The first thing Jim Hannigan became aware of was a whistle. Shrill, distant, it penetrated the shrouded depths of his awareness and drew him back to consciousness. His head banged like a horse had stomped on it and throughout his climb to wakefulness everything remained dark. He wondered if he had really woken at all but pain told him he had. He blinked, realizing after a throbbing moment that he was simply staring straight up into the cloud-blanketed night sky.

A peculiar vibration came from somewhere

beneath him. A distant rumble and chuffing reached his ears. The sounds of a train.

Another sound followed, a clanking thud. At first he wasn't certain what had caused it.

With an effort that augmented the pounding in his skull, he tried to sit up, discovering immediately that he could not. He attempted to move his legs, his arms; both wouldn't budge and his mind was still a bit too muddled to figure out why.

'Wake up, Mr Hannigan,' a voice came from somewhere near him. The voice sounded muffled, obviously disguised, though he felt certain it belonged to a man.

He lifted his head, eyes narrowing. Images stood out in shadowy relief now, none of them encouraging.

Ropes surrounded his torso, cinching his arms to his sides; his legs were bound together. Those ropes had been pounded into the wooden ties of a railroad track at his ankles and wrists, which explained why he couldn't sit up. The sound of a hammer hitting the spikes accounted for the clanking he'd heard. He twisted his head to see the glaring light of an approaching steam locomotive in the distance. The sight made his belly plunge. The conductor would never see him in time to stop the train. The situation would have struck him as comical had it not been so serious.

'You've got to be kidding. . . .' he mumbled, head coming back around to gaze up at a darkened figure now standing above him.

'It's appropriate, do you not think, Mr Hannigan?

How many of those tawdry dime novels have you starred in? Five, six? Now you will play an actual role in one.'

The voice, though disguised, carried a vaguely familiar quality, but Hannigan couldn't place it. The man – from the build it was indeed a man, nearly six feet tall, lanky – wore an executioner's hood and dark clothing.

'Who the hell are you?' he asked. The vibration beneath him grew stronger, the sounds of the approaching engine louder.

'I am your judge, your jury and your executioner, Mr Hannigan. I would have killed you outright but I've always had a taste for the theatrical. Besides, I hoped you might set an example for someone close to you. Perhaps then she'll see I was right all along, that weakness has no place in this world.'

'If I'm a dead man why not show me your face? Why hide it behind a mask?' Hannigan struggled against his bonds, though he knew it was useless. Escape was impossible. He could move only a matter of inches and would never be able to dislodge the spikes that pinned the ropes to the track, even given the time.

The figure laughed, a low whispery thing. 'If you had the time left you'd figure out who I am. Executioners always wear a mask, Mr Hannigan. Mine did, and so shall yours.' The figure bent and plucked the Bowie knife from Hannigan's boot sheath. He counted off ten paces, then jammed the blade into the gravel-bed between the tracks. 'So close, yet so far, as they say, Mr Hannigan. I bid you

41

adieu.' The figure walked away, vanishing into brush near the tracks. Hannigan heard no sounds of the man's departure through the undergrowth, only the oncoming train.

Twisting his head, he saw the train had gotten considerably closer. Sweat beaded on his brow, trickled down his temples. He had expected a trap, had taken precautions, but that Tootie was not here meant something had happened to delay her, perhaps permanently.

The thought giving him more worry than the notion of his own death, he struggled harder against the ropes. They wouldn't budge. He strained to pull his wrist free but failed to do more than scour flesh from his hide. A powerful jerk of his feet told him he'd never dislodge the spikes at his ankles, either. He was pinned, with no way of getting to the knife jammed into the ground ten paces away, and no way out.

'Christ. . . .' he muttered, heart starting to pound in rhythm with the throbbing in his skull.

The train whistle shrieked again. Gouts of steam puffed from the smokestack.

He pressed his eyes shut. There was nothing to do except await his fate. He'd never been a godly man but just in case he apologized for his sins. He didn't bother recounting them; they were legion, most lost to his memory, but he reckoned that if there were a god, that god knew the litany.

A new sound reached his ears, accompanying the shrillness of the train whistle, which was suddenly blowing with renewed intensity. A clanging bell, telling him the conductor had spotted something on the tracks and was issuing a warning, one useless to a man who couldn't move.

Hannigan's eyes opened. Light from the train now splashed over his trussed form and strained features. Brakes shrieked; sparks flew from locking wheels.

Then something else penetrated his dazed mind, nearly drowned out by the now-slowing engine. He wondered if, this close to death and suffering from the blow to his head, he wasn't merely hallucinating.

Hoofbeats. He swore he heard hoofbeats. A horse coming in at a gallop.

The hoofbeats suddenly stopped. Maybe he was indeed imagining them, for now all he heard was the desperate howl of a train struggling to stop before its wheels ground the life from the man tied to its tracks.

The light grew more intense, shining off the sweat running down his face.

Then an angel stood in that light above him, an angel with a frantic look on her face and desperate fear in her mahogany eyes. The angel knelt, yanked at one of the spikes holding him to the track.

'Jesus, I can't budge it!' Panic sang in her voice.

'Tootie, the knife—' He ducked his chin sideways. 'Ten paces down!'

Tootie stood, whirled, spotted the knife, now clearly outlined in the train light, sticking from the ground. She ran to it, doubled and gave it a yank, but it didn't come loose. Working the Bowie from side to side, she got it free after a few seconds.

She rushed back to him, dropped to his side, then

sawed at the rope between the spike and his wrist. Once through, she jumped over to the next, then to the ropes at his ankles.

The train was only a matter of a hundred feet away now, its brakes wailing like a dying animal. The roar of its approach had grown deafening.

Tootie jammed the knife between her teeth, scrambled off the track. Her fingers dug into the flesh beneath his arms, then she pulled. His left boot hooked the track, causing her nearly to lose her grip and fly backwards.

Time had run out. The train bore down like a giant devouring beast, shrieking and malign, mere feet away. She grunted, yanked. His boot jerked free, and his feet thudded off the track only an instant before the locomotive roared by.

After the train rushed past and receded into the distance, silence hung heavy, shroudlike. He heard her panting beside him as she sliced at the ropes pinning his arms to his side, then the ones binding his ankles.

'If I weren't so relieved I'd probably have the sense to be embarrassed,' he said, almost a whisper, as he sat up and rubbed circulation back into his limbs.

'Be embarrassed tomorrow.' She threw her arms around him, pulling him close. At that moment he reckoned he might have actually died because holding her was the closest thing to heaven a man like Jim Hannigan could ever hope to find.

'Somebody wanted to make an example of me, Tootie,' he said after long moments. 'This wasn't any ordinary play for revenge.'

She nodded, drew back, then rose. After she helped him to his feet he got a good look at her, saw the welts and puffed lips, bloody nose. He took her hand, turned it palm up.

'You're bleeding.'

She nodded. 'It's not deep. I'll live.'

'What happened?'

'I was watching in the alley like we arranged. Two men came out carrying you. I couldn't see their faces.'

'I saw them but I didn't recognize them either. Odd pair. I'll check with Widow Pass's marshal tomorrow and see what I can find.'

'Someone else was there, too, someone who expected me. She caught me by surprise before I could rescue you from those men.'

'She?'

Tootie frowned. 'You recollect that gypsy we waylaid in Angel Pass last fall?'

He nodded. 'Madam Mystique.'

'It was her. She was with those two men. I left her in the alley. We should go back and check, but I'd wager she's long gone by now.'

He looked off into the distance at the receding train. A peculiar feeling wormed its way into his being. Something that hooded figure had said about theatrics and weakness, added to the reappearance of the gypsy, brought a name to mind.

But that man was dead. . . .

'We'd best go have a look anyway,' he said, forcing the feeling down for the moment. He put his arm around her and they started walking towards her horse.

'You smell anything peculiar?' he asked, brow cinching.

'Like?'

He shrugged. 'Horse-dung, maybe. . . ?'

Tootie punched him in the arm.

CHAPTER FOUR

As Tootie del Pelado stepped from the Silver Spoon Café out into the morning sunlight, she found the light breakfast she'd just finished had done little to relieve two irritations prying at her mind. The first burr in her backside belonged to Jim Hannigan, whose stubborn insistence on putting himself in an unnecessarily dangerous position had nearly gotten his brains scattered across half the territory last night. She'd chastised him for that until his ears rang after they'd woken this morning, continuing from where she'd left off the night before. She wasn't finished with him yet, either, not by a damn sight. She wagered that that prospect accounted for his early start today and his decision to skip breakfast; but he couldn't avoid her forever.

If a poorer idea than walking into something he'd felt almost positive was a trap existed she hadn't encountered of it. She had told him so, too. Over and over. Before meeting Hannigan she had worked under cover long enough to know that subtlety beat the hell out of stumbling into situations blind. At least as far as getting run over by a train was

47

concerned. Times were changing; subterfuge was replacing the reckless, bull-ahead methods of the manhunter. She hoped he learned that before she was tossing a handful of dirt into his open grave.

'Ooohhh!' she blurted, a burst of anger flushing her cheeks with heat. He made her so, so, so . . . *peeled*!

The second thing that annoyed the hell out of her was the surprise and decidedly unwelcome appearance of the gypsy last night. When they'd returned to the alley behind the Regency, the woman had already high-tailed it, as Tootie suspected would be the case, but she bet that bitch-on-hoofs hadn't gone far.

Why was that woman in Widow's Pass? Revenge, obviously, but killing them for their part in arranging a few days' boarding at the Iron Bar Hotel seemed a trifle extreme. They had presented no charges that would stick, so she would have been released shortly after her incarceration. That she was here gave Tootie a niggling case of dread and a notion she damn well didn't care for – a notion pointing to a dead man.

'She's not working alone,' Tootie said under her breath, wrapping her arms about herself as she walked along the boardwalk.

A thief, a whore, a hellcat fighter, Mystique wasn't smart enough to be the brains behind any scheme luring Hannigan to Widow's Pass. No, someone else was pulling her strings.

Again dread whispered through her as a dark suspicion formed a link from Madam Mystique to a name she prayed she would never hear again.

'No . . .' she whispered, pausing on the boardwalk to stare out at the hardpacked street. 'He's dead. He has to be.'

She pushed the notion away, refusing to let the name touch her lips and conjure the waves of grief that came with it. That part of her life was over. It had to be. She didn't think she could face. . . .

A buckboard rattled past, jolting her from her thoughts. She stood there, a chill swelling in her heart, despite the warmth of the early-morning sunlight on her face. With a deep breath, she gathered her composure.

She had a job to do. That required an analytical mindset, at least until she knew for certain her suspicions were warranted, and despite her mere nineteen years she was an experienced professional. She was . . . strong.

Her first job, she decided, was to establish a list of places she might infiltrate to find a lead on the case. She spotted a handful of saloons, which usually would have been her first choice. In this case taking on the part of a bargirl was problematic. She couldn't work them all and she had little to go on for questioning bartenders and girls of the line. She could ask about new arrivals, possible whisperings about plots to bring down a well-known manhunter, but any errant piece of information she might pick up would cost her more time than they likely had. Whoever had called Hannigan here knew by now that the attempt on his life had failed, and would waste little time before attempting to rectify that mistake.

She wagered Madam Mystique would be itching to

get another shot at her, too, especially after coming out on the short end of their previous two encounters.

She sighed. That didn't leave many trails to follow, did it?

With a frown, she stepped off the boardwalk and drifted towards the Regency. Since that was where the attack had occurred, she could start by questioning the staff. Maybe she could ferret a lead to whoever had arranged for Room 10, though she had her doubts. Whoever secured the room had probably done so under an alias and would have been careful to leave no traceable leads. Still, it was worth a shot; sometimes outlaws got stupid or brazen and at the moment she couldn't think of a better plan.

As she approached the hotel she noticed two men shuffling from the alley that ran along its left side. They were lugging a blanket-wrapped body and endeavoring to appear as inconspicuous as possible, which, considering what they were carrying, proved impossible. Already a number of passers-by had spotted them and were pointing, shock on their faces.

Tootie made a beeline for the men, who had reached a wagon parked in front of the hotel. They unceremoniously heaved the bundled corpse into the back. The sound it made hitting gave Tootie a twinge of revulsion.

She got in front of one of the men and grabbed his sleeve. 'What happened?' The other man scrambled around the wagon and climbed into the driver's seat.

The man, short with a balding head and an eye

that tended to wander, peered at her. 'Who're you?'

'My name's Hannah Garrett. I'm a reporter. I came to this town to do a story about Widow's Pass for the Denver *Post.*'

The man frowned. 'No story here, miss.'

'I beg to differ, suh.' She tried her southern belle accent and hoped the man hadn't noticed she didn't have it a moment before. He didn't impress her as overly bright and she got away with it.

'Clerk got hisself stabbed. In the back room.'

'Jesus, Harley, shut the hell up, will ya?' the other man said, looking back over a shoulder. 'You know what that gal's gonna do with anything you tell her. She'll print it up in her paper, then no one will want to come here.'

Harley looked annoyed at his partner's reproach but Tootie gave him a sugary smile and he grinned.

'Just tellin' the truth, Bufus. Public has a right to know, ain't that right, miss?'

'That's right as rain, sugar.' Her smile turned sultrier and she ran a finger down the man's shirt front. 'Now why don't you tell little ol' me just what happened to that poor fella.'

'Harley!' the man in the driver's seat yelled.

'Close yer trap, Bufus,' Harley shot back, still grinning. 'Like I told yer, clerk got hisself kilt. Firs' time anything like this ever happened here, though lately. . . .'

'Lately what?' Tootie asked.

The man shrugged. 'Dunno, just lately I hear things 'bout folks, gals mostly, disappearin'. The marshal don't seem to care a lick, neither.'

A groan came from Bufus, who was clearly thinking his partner was going to get them both fired.

'Marshal?'

The man ducked his chin towards a building down the street, its large plate window sporting gilt lettering that said MARSHAL'S OFFICE. 'Marshal Hicks. He came in 'bout four months back after the old marshal died suddenly.'

'What'd he die of?'

'Stupidity, I reckon.'

'I declare, that's a right peculiar thing to die of.'

Harley shook his head. 'Not when yer wife catches you with a saloon girl. She put three bullets in his sorry hide, then tried to do the same to the gal, but some cowboys jumped her.'

'Any idea who might have killed this poor man?' She nudged her head toward the blanket-wrapped body.

'Nosiree, miss. The morning clerk found his body in the back room. No sign of who done the deed.'

'Anything else I should know?'

He shook his head. 'Just that I'm lookin' to court me a gal and you'd make a fine choice.'

She smiled, patted his cheek. 'Why, my kind suh, I do declare, I'd likely be too much for you to handle.'

'I'd be willin' to try.' He grinned, a lascivious light sparkling in his eye.

'I reckon you would, but one body a day's enough, don't you think?' She dropped the accent and turned away, then went to the Regency and disappeared inside, leaving the man staring after her.

It took about half an hour of questioning the staff

to establish exactly what she already knew – nothing. The ledger gave the Majenta de la Vaga name and nothing else. Room 10 proved empty, nothing disturbed, nothing left behind to indicate anyone was planning on returning. The day clerk could provide no further information about the murder other than the fact that he had discovered the body in the back room upon coming on duty. The wounds made a stabbing apparent but no knife had been found.

When she came out of the hotel the wagon was gone. She doubted she could learn anything from the body anyway. She stood there, hands on her hips, and blew out a frustrated sigh. She hated to a admit it but she was at a dead end.

She stepped off the boardwalk, intending to go back to her own hotel, a smaller affair a few blocks down in which they had rented a room late last night. Across the street a small store displayed some of its goods – fresh breads, pies and various baked goods – in baskets and bins on the boardwalk. A young woman – she couldn't have been more then sixteen or seventeen – stood pressed against the wall of the shop, which cornered an alley. Dressed in shabby clothing, she might have been mistaken for a boy, except for the fact that wisps of reddish-brown hair straggled from beneath a battered felt hat with a string that ran beneath her chin and enough breast strained at her grimy canvas blouse to make such a conclusion impossible. Her trousers, though baggy, did little to hide the fact that her hips were as curvaceous as those of a woman double her age.

Tootie noticed instantly that the girl was up to something. She could tell by the furtive glances she gave passers-by and the shopkeep sweeping the boardwalk, as well as the rigid stance of her frame as she tried to lean nonchalantly against the wall. Tootie stood still, observing her. The girl's attention was too focused on the bins of food for her to notice that she was being watched. The shopkeep finished sweeping, then entered the store, paying the girl no mind.

The girl made her move the moment the man went inside. She slipped from the corner, grabbed a loaf of bread, then scurried back into the alley and ran.

Tootie surveyed the surroundings, noting another alley a block down. She bolted across the street and headed for it, figuring she could cut the girl off if she came up that way or tried to escape down a back street.

On reaching the alley, she stopped, discovering she'd gotten lucky. The girl had her back pressed against a building and was tearing into the loaf of bread. Tootie eased into the alley, coming within five feet of the girl, who suddenly looked up, eyes flaring, body tensing to run.

Tootie's hand whipped up in a halting gesture. 'Wait, don't run! I won't hurt you.'

The girl hesitated, defeat washing into her eyes. 'You saw me steal this?' She held up the loaf of bread.

Tootie nodded. 'I saw you.'

The girl looked at the bread, then back to Tootie. A tear slipped from her eye and she quickly brushed it away. 'I can't pay for it.'

Tootie gave her a reassuring smile. 'I reckon you must have been desperate. I won't tell anyone, don't worry.'

The girl studied her, blue eyes narrowing. Tootie couldn't read what she was thinking, but saw fear and weariness on the girl's features.

'I was; desperate, I mean. I wouldn't have done it otherwise.'

'What's your name?'

The girl paused, nose crinkling. 'Druella. Druella Bradly.'

Tootie's smile warmed. 'I reckon the question, then, Druella Bradly, is why are you so desperate you're stealing bread?'

'Should be obvious. I was hungry.'

Tootie almost laughed. 'Yes, reckon that was obvious. You got folks?'

The girl stiffened, more fear swarming into her eyes. She remained silent.

Tootie held up her hand, palm up. 'Come. Let me buy you something to eat.'

'Why?' The girl's expression turned suspicious, intense. She appeared as if she were trying to peer into Tootie's soul, read her thoughts. 'Why would you do that? Less you want something from me, something bad.'

'I don't want anything from you, Druella. I'm a sucker for strays, I reckon, least that's what a certain fella I know says. Now, you got a choice, sweetie; you can take a chance with me and get some real food into your belly or I can leave you to that loaf of bread.'

The girl glanced at the loaf again, then back to Tootie. A moment later she tucked the bread beneath her arm, then came forward and accepted Tootie's hand.

Fifteen minutes later, after Tootie had stopped at the shop and paid for the loaf, they sat in the Silver Spoon café. The café was a small affair, with a dozen tables covered with blue-checked cloth and bright-yellow curtains. The scents of steak and peach pie filled the air.

Druella Bradly had doffed her hat and was devouring the plate of beefsteak and biscuits before her.

Tootie studied the girl, who was more a young woman, really. Druella had piercing blue eyes that reflected more pain than Tootie thought should be seen in anyone so young. She was a pretty girl, beneath the grime, with pale white skin and a smattering of freckles, a fine bone structure and, cleaned up, full lips that would drive the boys wild.

'When's the last time you had a decent meal?' Tootie asked.

The girl looked up, grabbed her cup of coffee and downed a huge gulp. She peered at Tootie, her expression a bit more trusting, but still retaining some suspicion. 'Been a spell.'

'I figured. You care to tell me why you're on the street stealing bread?'

'You promise you won't tell the marshal . . . or my pa?'

Tootie frowned. 'That depends on what you tell me. I can't make promises without knowing the details.'

The girl glanced out the window, dark emotions playing across her face. She seemed to deflate suddenly, as if every ounce of strength had deserted her. Tears filled her eyes when she looked back to Tootie, but didn't flow. 'I ran away . . . from my pa.'

Tootie nodded, took a sip of her own coffee. 'You got a good reason for doing that?'

Druella's eyes shifted as she paused. 'I got good enough reasons, I figure.' The girl suddenly unbuttoned the top part of her blouse and pulled it open enough so Tootie could see the livid bruises that covered the upper swell of her breasts.

'My god,' Tootie whispered, belly sinking. 'Your pa . . . did he do that to you?'

The girl rebuttoned her blouse and uttered a biting laugh. 'He did that. He does it once a week when he gets so drunk he doesn't feel like sticking his pecker in me.'

Something in Tootie's soul seemed to freeze over. 'Have you told the marshal about this?'

Druella's laugh turned more cynical. 'Marshal Hicks? He'd just join in.'

Tootie's brow furrowed. Everything in the girl's demeanor said she was telling the truth. 'Why are you still in town? Why not get as far away from here as possible? You must have kin somewhere?'

Druella swallowed hard, lower lip quivering. 'I got no one and nowhere to go. I reckon I'll have to go back to my pa soon, because no man'd ever want me now, not after the way he soiled me. I half-figured maybe I could just let myself, you know, starve to death, escape that way, but I was too much of a coward. I wanted to die, but couldn't do it myself.'

Tootie touched the girl's hand. Druella looked as if she would pull away, but didn't. Instead, a tear slipped from her eye and rolled down her cheek.

'How long has this been going on? How long has he. . . ?'

'Been laying with me? Two years, now, I reckon. Ever since my ma died.'

'How old are you?'

'Seventeen. Be eighteen in a few weeks.'

'You had any learnin'?'

She nodded, looked out the window again. 'I had some. Did more on my own. I figured maybe . . . maybe I could teach myself something that would help me get away from him, but a woman's got no real life after her pa takes away her . . . *gift*.'

Tootie gave her a reassuring smile. 'Your gift is who you are, Druella, not what you can give a man.'

She looked back to Tootie. 'That's easy for you to say, ma'am—'

'Please, call me Tootie.'

'That's easy for you to say . . . Tootie. You haven't been though what I have.'

'I could tell you what I've been through, but now isn't the time for *my* life story. Just trust me when I say I understand some of what you feel . . . and I can help you. I know a man—'

'No!' The girl suddenly yanked her hand away, fear flashing across her face. 'I won't do that, no matter how worthless I am. I won't do that.'

Tootie's face cinched. 'That's not what I meant, Druella. This man I know, he loves me. I work with him. We're . . . equals. He and I can help you.'

'What do you do? With this fella, I mean.' The girl's eyes cradled suspicion and Tootie reckoned she couldn't blame her. Her life up until now had done anything but foster trust.

'We have an agency. We hire out to help folks who need it. He's a manhunter and I worked for an investigation outfit before joining him.'

The girl gave her a cocked eyebrow. 'But you're a woman. They don't let women do that, do they?'

'Times are changing, honey.' Tootie smiled. 'Women can do some things a man never could. You wouldn't want to see my partner dressed as a bargirl or schoolmarm, let me tell you!'

The girl laughed, a bit strained but unbidden. Then her face turned serious again. 'Why?'

'Why what?'

'Why would you want to help me? You saw me stealing that bread. For all you know I might be lying to you about my pa.'

Tootie's gaze locked with hers. 'Bruises say different. And like I said, we help people. I reckon it's not always going to be the folks who hire us and we've got a duty to set some right things that need it.'

The girl struggled to keep her lip from quivering harder. 'You some kind of a nun or something?'

Tootie chuckled. 'Likely the furthest thing from it.' She paused. 'I know what I am going to ask you might be too much for you, considering what you've been through, but I am going to ask it just the same. I want you to trust me, let me help. I'm askin' for nothing in return and if you ever think anything's

59

different from the way I say it is you can always run away again. But if you let me help I can promise you that sonofabitch you got for a father will never touch you inappropriately again.'

The girl looked out the window for long moments, this time little emotion on her face, but her eyes roving constantly. Tootie wondered what she was thinking, how she was weighing the offer. When the girl turned back to her she could see she had won, at least for the moment, but not for the reason she had hoped. She had won because the girl looked utterly defeated. Druella had given up and whatever fate held in store with a stranger was likely no worse than what she would be going home to.

'All right, Miss Tootie. I'll trust you. I got nothing else.'

'You won't be sorry, Druella. I promise you.' Tootie stood, leaned over the table and wrapped her arms about the young woman. Druella didn't respond at first, then tentatively hugged Tootie back.

Tootie tossed some greenbacks onto the table. Druella stood, leaving the stolen bread and her hat on the table, tears shimmering in her eyes. Rising above the defeat Tootie now saw something else in the young woman's eyes: a glimmer of hope, determination.

Once on the boardwalk, Tootie's gaze scanned the street for her next destination. She turned to the girl, who somehow looked more fragile now, a dirty waif of a thing waiting for the wind to blow her in a direction. Her street demeanor had dissolved; she was just a lonely, abused young woman desperately looking to save herself from a path that would surely lead to ruin.

'Where's your pa's place?' Tootie asked, anger suddenly overflowing within her now that she had relaxed her guard after persuading Druella to trust her.

Fright jumped into Druella's eyes; she appeared on the verge of running. 'Why do you want to know that?' Her voice shook, followed by the rest of her body. Tootie placed a comforting hand on her shoulder.

'Like I said, my friend and I help folks. Your pa can't be allowed to get away with what he's done to you. I'll see to it he's punished.'

Druella grabbed Tootie's arm, her fingers digging in. 'Please, please don't go near him. You don't know what he's capable of.'

Tootie gave her a reassuring smile. 'Honey, I've seen men commit acts you wouldn't believe a body capable of. He's just another lowlife who needs to face up to his crimes and be taught he can't get away with them.'

The girl hesitated, then relaxed her grip on Tootie's arm. 'You . . . won't tell him where I am?'

'Never. You're not going back to him, Druella, not unless you want to.'

'I never want to see him again...unless he's swinging from a cottonwood. . . .'

That just might be an option, Tootie thought, but didn't say it. After the young woman gave Tootie the address, Tootie clasped Druella's hand and pulled her off the boardwalk. 'Come. . . .' She led her across the street to a dress shop. An hour later they came out, Druella clutching a paper-wrapped bundle that contained a new blue gingham dress.

They strolled back to the hotel, the tentative smile on Druella's face bringing a measure of warmth to Tootie's heart. It was only a first step for the young woman, but a big one, and Tootie prayed she'd stay on the trail until it took her where she wanted to go.

At the front desk, Tootie asked the clerk to send up a bath, then guided Druella up to the room. The room was large, better furnished than most places they had stayed in since she'd partnered with Hannigan, but modest compared to the Regency's lavishness. Gaslighting illuminated the room, which held a brass-framed bed, a bureau with a porcelain pitcher and basin, nightstand, two velvet-padded wing-back chairs and a writing table with a high-backed chair.

A small bar held a decanter with whiskey and glasses.

'I'm going to have a parley with that marshal about your pa,' Tootie said, after Druella had sat on the bed and torn the papering from her package. The young woman held up the dress, stared at it almost with reverence. She looked up at Tootie a moment later, frowning. 'He won't listen, Miss Tootie. He's a bastard. And even if he hears what you got to say he won't do a thing about it 'cept ask my pa how much he could have me for.'

Tootie nodded, lips a grim line. 'Believe it or not, you aren't the first to extol the marshal's virtues this morning. I'll see if I can get anywhere with him. If

62

not, my friend will take over. He's a bit less patient than I am.'

'What's your friend's name?'

'Hannigan. Jim Hannigan. You can trust him with your life, Druella. I have.'

A knock sounded on the door and Tootie went to answer it. Two men carrying an oblong steel tub stood in the hall. She gestured them in and they set down the tub, promising to return shortly with the hot water.

'Take your bath and get cleaned up, Druella. Don't go back out unless you're with me or Hannigan.'

The girl nodded, stood, then laid the dress out on the bed. 'Thank you, Miss Tootie,' she said, voice low. 'I don't know how I can ever repay you for all this.'

Tootie smiled. 'You don't have to, unless it's by living your life the way you want it to be lived.'

She left the young woman in the room, hoping she wouldn't simply run off the moment she had the chance.

CHAPTER FIVE

Tootie strode to the marshal's office, her anger at the man who called himself a father to the girl growing with each step. She forced herself not to think about the way that man had touched Druella, otherwise she might have gone straight to his homestead and put a bullet 'twixt his eyes without a shred of remorse.

Upon entering the marshal's office, she found the lawman sitting in a thick-padded chair behind his desk. He looked up at her, brow furrowing. Relatively young, he appeared about Hannigan's age, but a mean set to his eyes told her that that was where any similarity ended. Had she encountered him on the trail she might have labeled him a hardcase rather than a lawman. Outlaws had a figurative stink to them and this one had polecat hanging all over him in her estimation. Intuition warned her Druella was right, too: this man would show no sympathy for a young woman wanting to escape an awful situation.

'Help you?' His tone said: *Why the hell are you bothering me?*

She set her carriage with confidence. 'I've come to report a crime, Marshal.' Looking at the man gave her a twinge of unease, so her gaze skipped about the office. The room held three cells to the back, wall racks upon which rested rifles, and a table with a blue-speckled, enameled coffee pot. The odor of stale coffee and Durham permeated the air.

'That so?' Now his tone said he didn't give a damn. When she entered he had been busy staring off into space and was inclined to keep right on with that endeavor.

She forced herself to lock gazes with Hicks. Again she got an uneasy feeling about him. 'I've got a young girl at my hotel, name of Druella Bradly.'

The marshal shrugged. 'Your peculiar tastes ain't of much interest to me, 'less I'm involved.' The smile that came with the remark solidified everything she needed to know about the man. He was a tin-starred weasel and a useless peckerwood.

Ignoring him, she said: 'Her father took liberties with her, beat her, too. I want you to arrest him.'

'Now why in hell would I waste my time doing that?'

Tootie's brow crinkled. 'Think I just told you that.'

'No, you told me about a father who loves his daughter.'

Tootie's blood boiled and she suppressed the urge to scream at him. 'Didn't you hear what I just said? He took *liberties* with her.'

'Heard you just fine. If by liberties you mean he had her in a manly way, Miss—?'

'del Pelado. Angela del Pelado.'

'Well, Miss Angela del Pelado, nothing wrong with a father loving his daughter when he has a mind to.

65

I figure it brings a family closer. Poor Mr Bradly's wife passed on a couple years back from what I hear tell. A man gets lonely . . . hungry for the things a young woman can provide him.'

For a heartbeat she stood utterly stunned. Druella had told her this man would prove indifferent to her plight, but this . . . this condoning of such a *depravity* . . . she couldn't believe what she was hearing. She'd encountered some sick sons of bitches on cases, but this supposed man of the law might have given them a run for their money. 'You cannot be serious, Marshal. . . .'

He grinned, the grin of a coyote. 'But I am, Miss del Pelado. What goes on in a man's home is his own business and none of mine or yours. I've seen Miss Bradly. She's a young gal, right comely. She'll get over it and be all the better for what he's taught her.'

Tootie's eyes narrowed; for a moment she saw only red and imagined pulling the derringer from her skirt and shooting the man where he sat. Only a thread of control stopped her from doing so. Her voice lowered. 'I insist you arrest him for what he's done. He soiled that girl, and likely she'll be a life-time struggling with the nightmare of it.'

The marshal laughed and thudded his boots up onto the desk. 'Just who the hell are you, Miss del Pelado, to insist on me doing a damn thing in this town?'

'I work for an agency. I'm here on a case. You don't take action I'll fetch a territorial marshal to do your job for you.'

The marshal shifted his feet back off the desk,

then leaned forward. Some of the mocking in his expression had dissolved with her mention of a territorial marshal, but not all of it. 'What case might that be?'

'A telegram called my partner and me here to investigate a daughter's kidnapping.'

'Only kidnapped daughter I see in this town is Mr Bradly's. Suppose I arrest *you* for that?'

Tootie's voice didn't waver and she stared him straight in the eye, despite her revulsion. 'Try it, Marshal. You won't like the consequences.'

The marshal studied her, but didn't make a move to implement his threat. 'This partner of yours, who might he be? I assume it is a he or has the Women's Temperance League taken up detective work?'

'His name's Jim Hannigan. You might have heard of him.' The look that flashed across his eyes said he had and it was nothing he wanted on his doorstep.

'Get out of my office, Miss del Pelado, before I do decide to arrest you. And send that gal back to her pa. I won't ask nicely again.'

'You'll do nothing, then?'

'Not to Marcus Bradly.'

Tootie considered the situation, deciding that for the moment they were at an impasse and riling Hicks further would do neither her nor Druella any good. She wasn't done with the sonofabitch, though, not by a long shot.

Tootie left the office, heart pounding, blood racing. Frustration and anger made her gait stiff and her hands shake. She would not accept the marshal's decree and she refused to let Druella's father get away with what he had done. She gazed down the street in the direction of the address Druella had given her for her pa, impulse and emotion overwhelming her. She reckoned that that was her next stop and she was coddling just the right mood for it. If the marshal wouldn't to do anything about the man, she would handle him herself.

A door opened at the back of the marshal's office and a woman stepped into the room. Marshal Hicks looked over at her from where he'd been staring out the window at the del Pelado woman who had just stepped off the boardwalk and was headed, he guessed, toward the Bradly homestead. It didn't surprise him, despite his warning to her. She appeared the headstrong type, one who wouldn't veer from a goal once her mind was set on it. He'd been warned about that.

'You heard?' he asked the woman, who came up to his desk. His gaze remained fixed on the street beyond the window.

'I heard,' said Madam Mystique, folding her arms across her tan blouse. Bruises and scratches crisscrossed her face.

'You know which hotel she's staying at?'

'I know. Mr Rory spotted her and Hannigan coming out of it earlier this morning.'

'The Bradly girl is there. She's young, pretty.'

Madam Mystique smiled. 'I am sure Alejandro will be interested in her. I'll deal with Miss del Pelado afterward. I owe her some special attention.'

'Somethin' tells me she's not the type easily

handled.' He turned to the Mexican woman, a peculiar smile on his lips. 'Can see you already found that out for yourself, though.'

Anger flashed across Carmella's chocolate eyes. 'Shut the hell up, Hicks. Next time will be different.'

'Alejandro wants to deal with her himself—'

'I don't care what he wants. She's mine.'

He shrugged. 'It's your life. . . .'

In the hotel room, Druella Bradly sat in the tub, knees pulled up to her chest, arms wrapped about them, head down. She could not remember the last time she had taken a bath in peace. At home, she had been afraid to indulge in such a simple pleasure, for fear her father would gaze upon her nakedness the way he always did, then insist on. . . .

She shuddered, forcing the thought away.

The warm water felt like heaven. She had scrubbed the grime from her face and body, and now simply relished the water against her skin, the soothing effect it had upon her muscles and nerves. Her red-brown hair cascaded over her shoulders now that she was minus the battered hat. Without the dirt she looked much more like a beautiful young woman with her whole life ahead of her than the street waif Tootie had befriended, though she doubted she could ever scour the filth of her pa's touch from her soul.

A tear slipped down her cheek, dripped into the water. She watched the ripples it made, and wondered what ripples her pa's sick needs would send through her life to come. And perhaps now she *did* have a life to come, a true one. Tootie had been so kind to her, though she couldn't understand why anyone would want to help a girl in her situation. If her father ever found out he might kill Tootie; Druella knew the rage that consumed him when things didn't go his way. She should have told her such, made her understand how much of a bastard Marcus Bradly really was, but selfishness had overcome her, *hope* had overcome her. If there was some chance, no matter how small, she could escape the hell she'd been forced to live for the past two years, she had to take it. She couldn't spend another night sleeping on the ground, the bugs and snakes crawling into her trousers and shirt while she slept. Nothing remained for her if this turned out to be something different from what Tootie assured her it was.

A sound came from the door, startling her from her thoughts. She looked up through bleary eyes to see the door opening. A gasp came from her lips and she drew her knees up tighter against her body. A woman stood in the doorway, a Mexican woman with a glint in her eyes that told Druella everything she needed to know about her. This woman was not like Tootie; this woman was the Devil's plaything. Behind the woman stood two smallish men, their faces smug, almost eager, though neither impressed her as the type who would be interested in the nakedness of a young woman.

'Well, what a pretty little thing you are,' said the woman, who came into the room. She set the rifle she was holding against the bureau next to the door.

70

'Alejandro will be most pleased.' The woman went to the bed, picked up the gingham dress and looked it over.

'Who are you?' Druella asked.

'Get out of the tub and put this on,' ordered the woman, ignoring her question. The two men came into the room, shutting the door behind them. 'If you scream or make any attempt to escape, I'll kill you and the woman who brought you here.'

Druella didn't move. Fear froze her where she sat.

The Mexican woman threw down the dress, whirled and grabbed her beneath both arms. With strength that Druella reckoned belonged to a man, the woman hauled her from the tub. Druella tried to kick and struggle loose, but the woman was too strong and the two men jumped in to help her.

The Mexican woman stepped back, leaving her in the grip of the men.

'Get her dressed and take her to Alejandro. I have business to attend to with her savior. . . .'

The Bradly homestead was a run-down affair at the far edge of Widow's Pass. Likely one of the few holdover shacks from the town's silver-mine era, it looked like a wart on the hand of a piano player compared to the newer buildings that had been erected around it. Shudders dangled, boards were splintered and garbage congregated about the place. The roof sagged so much she wondered how it had ever made it through the winter without caving in. A number of the windows showed broken glass and Tootie felt even worse for the young woman who'd been subjected to living in those conditions.

She surveyed the place for signs of life; everything appeared serene, no one about. With a deep breath she approached the front steps, which were broken and riddled with termites. As her heart began to pound her hand went to the derringer in her skirt pocket, then came back out to knock on the door. She couldn't let her anger overwhelm her good sense. She had little idea what she would to say to the man but she needed a level head, no matter how much she wanted to put a bullet in his no-good hide.

No answer came to her first knock, so she pounded harder.

With that, she heard footsteps echo from within. The door jerked open. The man who stood there stank of old booze and too long without a bath. He wore a torn, stained undershirt and trousers that hung too far south of where they should have. Disheveled hair, greasy, long unwashed, peppered with gray, hung over his forehead. Stubble covered his weak chin. He peered at her, eyes webbed with red, bleary.

'Whatchu want?' His voice came slurred but a lusty glint sparked in his eyes as his gaze raked the young woman standing on his threshold. He was drunk, but not *that* drunk.

Tootie's hand shot out, taking him completely by surprise. She shoved him backwards into the house and he nearly lost his balance and went over backward. He managed to stay upright, but anger quickly wiped the lust from his face. So much for level-headedness, she thought. Where this man was concerned, she reckoned she had little control over her temper.

She glared at him, disgust welding to her face. 'I came to talk about your daughter, you lowly sono-fabitch.'

He sobered nearly all the way now, wiped drool from his lips. 'Druella? What the hell business you got with her?'

Tootie's voice remained cold, damning. 'You beat her. You touch her in ways no father should ever touch a daughter. That waste of a marshal wouldn't do anything about it but I'm here to let you know I intend to see to it you answer for your crimes. And if you ever go near her again I'll take a rusty knife to your southern parts, you understand?'

Crimson flooded the man's cheeks. She could tell instantly he wasn't the type to accept ultimatums from a creature as lowly as a woman; she almost laughed.

'Who the hell you think you are, comin' in here and tellin' me what I can and can't do with my daughter, you goddamn whore?'

The sound of his voice crashed like thunder, but she refused to let it intimidate her. 'I'm someone you're going to have to answer to if you ever get near that girl again. I'm tellin' you once, stay the hell away from her and pray to whatever devil you got I don't put a bullet in your ugly hide just for the satisfaction of it.'

The man laughed then, an obnoxious, grating sound that brought a measure of fury to her she couldn't deny.

'She wanted it, you dumb cow. She begged me for

it. She couldn't wait for me to come into her bedroom at night and stick my—'

Tootie's fist slammed into his mouth, cutting off what he'd intended to say.

Marcus Bradly's head snapped back, but he didn't go down. She had hoped he would. He drew the back of his hand across his mouth, wiping away a dribble of blood.

He laughed, mocking her, then grabbed his crotch. 'You're gonna beg me for it, too, you dumb whore. You're gonna love what—'

She hit him again and it felt damn good. She heard a satisfying snap of cartilage in his nose. Blood sprayed from his nostrils and he let out a grunt, staggered slightly.

'Why, you goddamn—'

Tootie gave him a grim smile. 'Some folks just never learn, do they?' She hit him a third time. His head rocked and a light in his eyes blinked off, then back on.

He made a grab for her, tried to get his hands around her throat. She sidestepped, sweeping up her foot then whisking it back to connect with the back of his left calf. His leg went out from under him and his arms windmilled as he flew backward.

He hit the floor hard, flat on his back, staring up, a dazed expression in his eyes. She kicked him square in the teeth. Blood spattered from his lips. He panted, a gurgling sound coming from his throat.

Tootie leaned over him, jammed a high-laced shoe into his chest, digging hard with the heel.

'You listen and you listen good, you stupid sono-

74

fabitch. Stay away from Druella or I'll come back and finish the job. I might even bring my friend with me; he isn't quite as gentle as I am.'

Marcus nodded. She withdrew her foot, backed away. He made no effort to get up.

Once she was outside she headed back into the town, only moderately satisfied with her encounter with Druella's father. She had let him off easier than she would have liked. She would have preferred filling him full of lead but that might have been difficult to explain to the marshal after making accusations against Bradly. In this town she had to be careful until she knew whether the lawman was just indifferent or vindictive.

On the positive side, she reckoned Bradly would stay away from his daughter now. Men like him were basically cowards who preyed on those who were weaker, but who shied away from those able to defend themselves. She wasn't finished with him yet, however. He needed to answer for what he had done to the girl, preferably at the end of a rope.

Barely completing the thought, Tootie dived sideways. A glint from a rooftop across the street had caught her eye and she reacted purely by instinct. A split second later a shot thundered through the street.

Lead plowed into the side of a building with a spray of slivers. A hole showed in the wall; had she not moved that hole would have been in her chest.

She crouched behind a rain barrel, gaze lifting in the direction from which the shot had come. She knew it couldn't be Bradly who'd fired at her; he was likely still pissing himself on the floor of his cabin. That left the unknown person who had summoned Hannigan to this town, or the gypsy, looking to get even for her thrashing in the alley last night. She bet on the gypsy.

Another glint of sunlight flashed from a rifle barrel. A second shot rang out. With a *thuck*, a hole appeared in the rain barrel and water spouted onto the boardwalk.

Searching for better cover, Tootie spotted a wagon a half-dozen feet away and bolted for it. The barrel wouldn't provide enough protection from a rifle and she had only a derringer, nothing with enough range to hit a bushwhacker on a rooftop.

A shot snipped at her heels as she reached the wagon and got behind it. Two more bullets gouged chunks from the vehicle's side.

Throughout the street women screamed and scrambled about. Men raced from the boardwalks, dragging their wives into buildings.

No more shots came, which was a blessing, because with so many people in a panic a stray bullet might hit one of them.

Tootie, glancing up, caught a glimpse of the gypsy spinning and fleeing from the rooftop. Her opportunity to kill Tootie had passed for the moment and she knew it. She was concentrating on escape.

Tootie raced across the street, rebounding from townsfolk who stumbled into her path. She hoped to head off the gypsy before she made her escape, but soon discovered it was too late. Madam Mystique had climbed down from the rooftop and vanished along a back street. Tootie spent another half-hour search-ing but to no avail.

Heading back towards the hotel, Tootie frowned and wiped her damp palms on her skirt. The blatant daylight attempt had shaken her a bit. She would have to be more careful, more alert, because next time that woman likely wouldn't miss.

CHAPTER SIX

Jim Hannigan didn't like the thoughts coming together in his mind. The telegram calling him to Widow's Pass, the theatrical style of the attack on him last night, combined with the appearance of the gypsy, all pointed to one man, a man six months in the grave.

If that man had somehow escaped his punishment. . . .

Christ, he hoped not. That case had put Tootie through hell. She'd dealt with enough grief over it; she didn't need to relive the events of Angel Pass.

He was jumping to conclusions, he told himself. He had no proof, just suspicions and tenuous threads. That meant that learning the facts of what had happened after they left Angel Pass was first on his agenda.

He headed for the telegraph office, alert for any sign of a threat. After what had occurred last night he wasn't inclined to take chances. While the morning looked serene, whoever had tried to kill him was still an unknown and could hide anywhere amongst the townsfolk, lurk around any corner. He saw no sign of the two peculiar hardcases who'd waylaid him or the gypsy, but that didn't mean he could let his guard down. He noted the marshal's office a block down from the telegram office; he would make that his second stop after wiring his Pinkerton friend. Perhaps there he could pick up a lead to any suspicious activity leading up to his arrival in Widow's Pass.

The telegraph operator looked up from his desk as Hannigan entered, gave him a slight nod. With the stub of a pencil provided on the counter, Hannigan wrote out his message on a slip of paper. The operator took his message, glanced over it, then nodded. Hannigan paid the telegraph man, then left, hoping the answer that came back wasn't the one he expected.

Outside again, the sun warming his face, he found his mind wandering towards thoughts unrelated to the present case. He'd been doing a lot of pondering over the winter. They'd had fewer cases in the cold weather and he'd spent more time with the woman he called his partner. But that wasn't the proper word, was it? Not any longer. She'd become so much more than that. Their relationship had grown closer, their bond stronger. He reckoned he'd caught himself considering things a manhunter normally refused to entertain. His calling, chasing down outlaws, came with certain complications not conducive to the idea that had taken hold in his mind. Enemies might strike at her to get to him and asking her the question simmering in his mind wouldn't make that situation a lick better. Fact was, it might make her even more of a target.

But she was already a target. Last night had made that plain. So that argument and any other he cared to entertain – he'd certainly run through the litany of them – didn't really stand up when it came to the final tally. He'd never dreamt he could feel anything as powerful as the emotions she brought out in him, emotions he'd eventually begun to accept instead of fight. He sighed a resigned sigh. He had never planned for a woman, for emotional attachments. Such things weren't for Jim Hannigan.

At least until Angela del Pelado stepped into his life. He loved her. Nothing could ever change that now. And despite the love she had confessed for him, he wagered one day soon she would make him face a choice: her or the trail. She would be his partner for life if he asked, but womenfolk didn't live with unspoken promises and steady ridin', the way a man did. They were peculiar creatures, he reckoned.

Settling down. It came down to that, didn't it? But could a man who had spent his life alone on the trail ever submit himself to a normal life? Did he have to, or could things go on the same between them, even if he went through with what he was considering?

Well, maybe for a spell, but she would likely want the next step, perhaps not immediately, but someday. Hell, the thought of young'uns made his belly tumble, but since he'd taken her to his bed over six months ago, he'd best be prepared to deal with the possibility.

He sighed, coming from his thoughts as he reached the marshal's office. He wiped his suddenly damp palms on his bibshirt, glad to turn his mind back to the case for the time being.

He found the marshal standing at the window, staring out. The lawdog didn't bother to acknowledge him when he came in.

'Marshal?' Hannigan closed the door, then doffed his hat, which he'd gone back into the hotel to collect last night after they'd searched the alley for the gypsy.

'I saw you heading here, Mr Hannigan. What do you want?' The man's tone carried a belligerent ring.

'You know me by sight?'

The marshal didn't turn from the window. 'Saw your likeness in a paper. Got a visit from your partner a short while ago, too.'

Hannigan's eyes narrowed. 'Tootie came here?'

'Tootie?' The man glanced at him for the first time, puzzled. 'Angela, she said her name was.'

Hannigan nodded. 'She told you about the attack last night then, the case we're working on?'

'She mentioned a case, nothin' about an attack. She has a big mouth.'

'She doesn't take cowflop from anyone, if that's what you mean.'

'I suppose. Tell her to leave the Bradly situation alone, Mr Hannigan. She don't belong sticking her nose in it. In fact, she don't belong sticking her nose in anything in this town and neither do you.' The lawman's tone came with a hint of a threat.

Hannigan had no idea what he meant by the Bradly situation, but he would find out from Tootie when he saw her.

'A fake telegram brought me to Widow's Pass, Marshal. A woman named Majenta de la Vaga claimed to need my services. When I went to meet her I got waylaid by two hardcases and a gypsy woman. There was a fourth person, too, but he wore a mask.'

'Did he now?' The marshal uttered a contemptuous chuckle. 'I suppose this fantasy has some motive?'

'At the moment I'm not sure of that. Revenge, I expect.'

The marshal's brow lifted and he gave a short nod. 'Why did you come here, then?'

'I was hopin' to look through your dodgers, see if I could pinpoint those two men. Also reckoned you could tell me whether anything unusual has been going on in this town, maybe within the past six months or so.'

'Six months, Mr Hannigan? Any reason for that particular time period?'

'Reckon that's the time frame I'm looking at if what I got in mind comes to pass.'

'And what might that be?'

'Best I keep that to myself till I know for certain.'

'Nothing going on in this town for the past six months or otherwise, Mr Hannigan. You wasted your trip.'

Hannigan ignored the comment. 'You been marshal here all that time?'

'No, only for the past four months. Former marshal met with an unfortunate accident at the hands of his wife. Reckon he should have been more careful where he dipped his wick.'

Tension shortened the muscles on the back of Hannigan's neck. 'I get the notion you're being deliberately unhelpful, Marshal.'

'That so?' The marshal locked gazes with him. Hannigan saw no back-down in the man's eyes. 'Maybe it's because I don't cotton to your murderin' type runnin' loose in my town. Maybe it's because you and your big-mouthed partner aren't wanted here. Frankly, I ain't the least bit surprised someone attacked you. Likely decent folk don't want a killer in their midst and decided to do something about it.'

Hannigan suppressed the urge to take a swing at the man. He was having a hard time reading him, his motives. The lawdog might be against manhunters or simply covering for some deeper motive. 'Those men who attacked me weren't decent folk, and neither is the woman with them. The woman, at least, belonged to a group who kidnapped innocent children and murdered honest men. I was lured here for a reason. I'd appreciate it if you helped me find out why.'

The marshal uttered a small laugh, then went to his desk and lowered himself into his thick-padded chair. 'Mr Hannigan, I wouldn't lift a finger to help your type, make no mistake about that. So you best just ride off to wherever the hell you came from and take any trouble you brought to this town with you.'

Hannigan frowned, irritation prickling the hairs on the back of his neck. 'I take it you won't give me access to your dodgers?'

The marshal smiled. 'You take it right.'

Hannigan set his hat on his head, for the moment accepting the impasse with the lawman. 'Likely I'll be visiting you again real soon, Marshal. Hope when I do you like being more helpful.'

'And if pigs had wings, Mr Hannigan. . . .'

Hannigan didn't reply. Battling his frustration, he left the office. After he'd stepped outside he glanced back to see that the marshal had returned to the window. The man gave him a smug smile.

The marshal might have been crooked, Hannigan thought. Then again, he might simply have been the type who didn't appreciate manhunters riding roughshod in his town. Too many of Hannigan's contemporaries carried reputations on a par with John Wesley Hardin's and weren't welcomed by the law.

With a sigh he made his way along the boardwalk, wondering about the marshal's remarks concerning Tootie. What had she gotten herself into? He considered returning to the hotel to find out before investigating the area around the tracks for signs pointing to his masked attacker's trail, but after brief debate, decided against it. He didn't need another lecture.

He started toward the edge of town, in the direction of the railroad tracks, but a moment later slowed to a leisurely stroll when he became aware of two men shadowing him. From their lack of subtlety he pegged them as rank amateurs and no real threat. He stopped, studied their reflection in a store window as he pretended to look over a new saddle. Average in appearance, both appeared to be ranch workers, their faces fraught with looks of trepidation and worry, but no malice.

He turned and confronted them. Both stopped in unison, startled to be caught in the act.

'Gentlemen,' he said with a slight nod.

'Mr Hannigan . . .' the one on the left said, voice low, shaky. 'We mean you no harm.'

'I figured as much from the delicate way you were stalking me.'

The one on the right laughed an uneasy laugh and both men appeared to relax a measure.

'My name's Hanly,' the one on the right said. 'And this is Borden. We hoped to talk to you a moment.'

'But we weren't sure how to approach you,' Borden said.

Hannigan shrugged. 'Best way is to say what you got to say straight out, I reckon.'

'You have quite a reputation, Mr Hannigan,' Borden said. 'Your picture's—'

'Been in the paper, I know. The bane of my life at the moment.' Hannigan smiled, putting the men further at ease.

'We want to hire you, Mr Hannigan,' Borden said. 'Hanly and I got together all our savings. We hope it's enough. We hear you hire for vengeance and we just might need ourselves some.'

'We're hoping we don't, mind you,' Hanly added quickly. 'But. . . .'

Hannigan nodded. 'Suppose you tell me why you require my services.'

Hanly shifted feet, looked at the ground, then back up to him. 'We've both got – *had* – daughters,

85

Mr Hannigan. Up until a few weeks ago.'

Hannigan's belly cinched. He knew what was coming and it did nothing to allay his suspicions about the person who had lured him here. 'What happened two weeks ago?'

Borden cleared his throat, lips quivering. 'They vanished, Mr Hannigan. Like they'd just stepped off the earth. My daughter and Hanly's, they were friends. They went to the spring dance together. They were helping out the church. But they never came home. Folks saw them leave together but that was the last that was seen of them.'

Hannigan sighed, the cinching in his belly getting tighter. 'You talk to the marshal about this?'

Hanly gave a laugh of contempt. 'That lawman's a worthless piece of—'

'Hanly,' Borden said. 'That won't help. Suffice to say he's been of no assistance, Mr Hannigan. And when I spotted you in town earlier this morning I went and got Hanly. We went to the bank and got this.' Borden reached into his pocket and pulled out an envelope, passed it to Hannigan.

Hannigan opened the envelope, peered inside. A thin stack of greenbacks showed, likely all these men had to their name and from the looks of them they had worked damn hard to come by it.

Hannigan peered at them, saw the pain in their eyes, and nodded. 'I can't make any promises, gentlemen, but I'll do my best to bring your daughters back. If I can't do that, I'll try to bring you whoever . . . well, let's just wait on that part until I know something for sure.'

Hanly looked ready to collapse with relief. 'Thank you, Mr Hannigan. Thank you so much. After the time we had with the marshal we thought there was no hope at all. Now we got some.'

Hannigan nodded. 'Met your marshal a few minutes ago. Reckon I didn't get the best impression.' Hannigan handed the envelope back to Hanly. Hanly accepted it, confusion crossing his face.

'But I thought you said you'd take the case. . . .' His voice was laced with disappointment.

'I did, Mr Hanly. But you can't afford me. Keep your money. Buy your daughters new dresses when I bring them back.'

'When?' Borden's voice quivered with hope.

Hannigan smiled. 'Like to think positive, Mr Borden. Lady friend of mine seems to be rubbing off on me.'

Hannigan left the two men staring after him as he resumed heading for the tracks. Two young women, missing. The pattern resembled the one in Angel Pass, and that didn't give him any hope that he'd made a mistake in his suspicions. In Angel Pass children, boys, had vanished. Here, young women had gone missing, but the person he had in mind would likely change methods to keep the law from connecting the dots back over six months.

Ten minutes later found Jim Hannigan at the railroad tracks outside of town. He glanced along them in either direction. No trains at the moment and he reckoned he suddenly had a whole new disdain for the vehicles. Man was meant to travel by horse, anyway.

Thick brush surrounded most of the track and pebbles covered exposed ground. The pebbles were disturbed in numerous areas, but not in a manner to indicate the passage of one person. He scoured the surroundings, finding nothing solid in the way of clues pointing to his attacker's escape path.

He paused, gaze roving. The attacker had fled into the brush but that covered a wide expanse. The hooded man could have traveled in any direction or simply come back out a ways down. The brush was scrabbly, low. Perhaps half a mile beyond the growth stood the hulk of the deserted silver-mine baron's mansion.

Jim Hannigan spent another few minutes searching the grounds, to make certain he hadn't missed anything, then drifted into the brush, bending slightly, eyes studying each leaf for signs of passage. He noted tiny gaps where leaves had been pulled from branches, but the ground was hard, held no footprints.

A hundred feet in, the growth thickened and the ground became carpeted with small leaves and sticks. With the lack of sign Hannigan saw only one option: continue in a straight line and hope the killer had not veered.

He paused, swiping a fly from his face, gaze traveling to the mansion in the distance. By now his attacker surely had come back to check his handiwork and discovered Hannigan had survived, so if the hooded man had been hiding out there, he had likely moved on. But he could not afford to pass up any options and outlaws were a cocky lot.

He headed for the mansion, gaze alert, sweeping the grounds as he approached. He spotted nothing threatening, no sign of life or recent habitation. Close up, the house appeared in sorrier disrepair than he'd expected. The mansion itself sprawled in peculiar directions, a nightmare of design. The lack of upkeep had done nothing to improve its inelegant lines. Shutters dangled, slats broken; boards hung loose and widows were fractured or missing panes together. Shrubbery had overrun the yard, jutting up through the walkway stones, which were thick with moss. Shrubs grew through cracks in the boards of the porch that ran the length of the stone-and-board mansion. He saw rats scurry along the stone base of the house, one dragging the corpse of some mangled smaller animal. Termites had chewed up great portions of siding. In its day, he supposed, the place had been a sight, the envy of all, but now it was the stuff of ghost stories, ruined prosperity and forgotten dreams.

He moved up to the porch, placed a boot on the bottom step, testing it. The broads were sagging, rotting, and the step creaked under his weight, but he judged it solid enough to support him. He climbed the steps slowly, each groaning, creaking, but holding. Pausing at the top, he studied every nook and cranny for lurking attackers, but no sign of anyone or any recent activity was in evidence.

He remained alert just the same, ready to go for his Peacemaker, positive other ways into the mansion existed and anyone hiding out would likely avoid the front door.

He crossed to the door, gripped the handle. The door groaned and creaked as he forced it inward, confirming the entrance had not been used in ages.

The mansion's interior was in a worse repair than the exterior. A vestibule branched to a huge drawing room on the left and a study on the right. A central grand staircase led to the second floor. Moldering blue velvet drapes hung half-off their mountings and collapsing furniture occupied both rooms. Varmints and insects had made short work of the wooden banisters and moldings; spiders had nested so liberally that great shrouds of webbing clogged most corners and blanketed the chandeliers hanging in the vestibule and drawing room. He spotted arachnids nearly the size of pie-plates skittering over the webs. He hoped he didn't stumble across any snake nests in the place. He didn't mind spiders but snakes were another matter.

He moved into the drawing room, listening intently for any noises that indicated a presence: a caught breath, a rustle of clothing. The only sound came from the breeze whining through cracks in the windows and the occasional skittering of rats. Mold covered great portions of the walls and stones were falling from the crumbling fireplace. A mahogany bar, thick with dust, held decanters and glasses, all layered in gray. A roach ran along the bartop and another crunched beneath his boot.

'Christ,' he mumbled. The place gave him an eerie feeling. He didn't believe in spooks but if any place were a candidate for a haunting this one qualified.

It took fifteen minutes to search the house, but he found no one. He saw evidence of scuffing feet in the dust in the drawing room and various other rooms but much could be attributed to animals making the place their own. At one point a large rodent of some sort scurried out from behind a dilapidated sofa and startled the hell out of him. If anyone had been using the place as a headquarters they appeared to have moved on.

In the pantry he discovered a trapdoor that he figured led to a root cellar. He yanked on the metal ring handle but the door wouldn't budge. He gripped it with both hands, spread his legs for leverage and pulled harder. The door remained stubborn. Stuck from years of disuse, possibly, it would take some prying to get it up. He'd have to come back with tools for that. He noted nearly no dust on the pantry floor, which made him suspicious, since the rest of the house was covered with it. Someone might have gone over the room, or, since the room was closed off and had no windows, perhaps dust hadn't accumulated in here. He noticed the shelves held old foodstuffs: rusty cans, boxes and empty grain-sacks, a few small bones, but nothing indicated the storage of fresh food for anyone hiding out.

He backed from the room and made his way to the front of the house. While it did not surprise him that the place was empty, he couldn't shake the feeling that if someone weren't here now they had been recently. With little evidence to support the notion, it was just his manhunter's sixth sense telling him it was the most logical place for his attacker to have hidden out, but that seldom failed him. He would come back and force open that root-cellar door to remove any remaining doubt, but for now his search was finished.

In the mansion's root cellar, Alejandro del Pelado kept his fingers clamped about the metal ring on the underside of the trapdoor until he heard Hannigan's bootfalls recede from the room. He was poised on the ladder leading to the door, and had thrown a bolt he'd installed underneath for just such an exigency. The bolt wouldn't keep the door from rattling and making it obvious it was locked from beneath, so he had needed every bit of strength to hold it still while the manhunter yanked on it from above. His arm ached from the strain and sweat poured down his face. Since he had the Bradly girl secured in his other arm, hand over her mouth, the task had been doubly hard.

With him in the cellar were the two effeminate hardcases, each standing beside a young woman sitting against the stone wall, their ankles and wrists bound, gags in their mouths. In each man's hand was a board, poised to strike should either girl make a sound. That threat had been the only thing keeping Druella Bradly from struggling or trying to scream.

A low-turned lantern burned on a table in the small square room. The table held scraps of bread and a pitcher of water; he needed to keep the girls alive until he sold them to the men riding up from Mexico next week.

Alejandro came down the ladder, glanced at his

men, then dragged the girl to a corner and hurled her to the ground. She gathered her dress about her legs and stared up at him in spite.

'You won't get away with this,' she said, murder in her tone.

'I already have, Miss Bradly. Now keep your mouth shut, please. You're not the virgin these other two are, so your value to me is negligible. I won't hesitate to put a bullet between your eyes if you give me any trouble.'

Druella Bradly glared but said nothing further.

'Tie her up and gag her,' he ordered the other men, who nodded in unison. 'We don't need her squawking if Hannigan comes back. I'll meet him on my terms, not his.'

Alejandro went back to the ladder, climbed it, then threw the bolt. He eased the door up and peered into the darkened pantry.

Hannigan was gone. Alejandro reckoned it was damn lucky that that gypsy hadn't decided to come traipsing back in while the manhunter was searching the place. In fact, after what Mr Rory and Mr Ryan had told him, he would have to deal with her when she *did* get back. He'd gotten damn tired of her insubordination, even if she had saved his life. And if she had killed his sister and deprived him of the chance of doing so, the way Hannigan had robbed him of avenging his parents' deaths, he would make Carmella's demise a most extended and unpleasant one.

CHAPTER SEVEN

When Tootie returned to the hotel room she discovered the door ajar. A shiver of warning skittered down her spine and her hand went to the derringer in her skirt pocket. She pressed herself against the wall to the left of the door and listened. No sound came from within the room; that worried her all the more. She'd told Druella to stay put and unless the girl had run back to her father, which Tootie doubted, something had happened. Her intuition told her it was something bad.

With her free hand she sent the door swinging inward. Nothing happened. No shots came from within, no sounds of movement.

Heart thudding in her ears, she counted off twenty seconds, then edged her face around the jamb and peered into the room. At a glance, it appeared empty. The tub still sat in the middle of the room but it was empty. Druella Bradly was nowhere in sight.

She eased into the room, finger ready on the trigger, but her caution proved unnecessary. A quick search proved the room to be vacant.

She noted the dress was also gone. Druella's dirty

clothing lay in a pile on a chair. Tootie pocketed the derringer and went to the tub, where she knelt and studied the floor. Puddles, spaced at haphazard intervals, told her the girl probably hadn't left the tub under her own power. An uneven wet trail led to the bed. Nothing else appeared disturbed but Tootie felt certain the girl had been abducted.

But by whom, and why? How would anyone know which hotel she and Hannigan had registered at? Which room they were staying in? The marshal couldn't have come to take the girl back to her father, because though she'd mentioned to him that the girl was at the hotel, she hadn't told him which one.

Had Mystique or one of the men who'd attacked Hannigan last night followed them to the hostelry? Learned the room number? Even so, why kidnap the young woman? She had no relation to the case.

A sound jerked her from her thoughts and she whirled to see Jim Hannigan standing in the doorway, concern on his face.

'What happened?' he asked.

'I met a girl. . . .'

He nodded. 'I heard. Marshal said something about it, but I had no idea what he was talking about.'

'He's a sonofabitch.'

He gave her a small smile as he stepped into the room. 'You'll get no argument from me on that point. Suppose you sketch the details.'

Tootie explained how she had caught the girl stealing food and befriended her, brought her back to the room.

'I left her here with a new dress and a bath. The dress is gone and so is she. I'm certain someone took her against her will.'

He glanced at the floor about the tub, then towards the bed and she knew he was studying the water marks. 'Intuition, or you going by the trail of water?'

'Someone pulled her out of the tub, dragged her to the bed, I figure.'

He nodded, kneeling and eyeing the water marks more closely. He looked up at her. 'Who would know we're here?'

'The gypsy or the men who attacked you, I'm guessing. Somebody must have dogged us last night.'

He straightened. The look on his face told her he could read her raw emotions and didn't care for what he saw. The young woman's plight had affected her, made the case personal and it worried him because it might compromise her judgment and get her killed. But he didn't say it and she was glad.

Without a word, he left the room, returning a few moments later.

'Where did you go?' Her brow crinkled.

He closed the door. 'Checked with the clerk. He said a friend of yours came in this morning and asked for your room number. This friend said she wanted to surprise you.'

Her stomach sank. Now she was sure the young woman hadn't left under her own power. 'He describe this woman?'

'Mexican, chest big enough for two. Said two

Nancys accompanied her.'

'Jesus . . .' Her lips pressed into a tight line and she wrapped her arms about herself. 'Why take Druella? She's got nothing to do with this case. They must know that.'

'Wrong place at the wrong time, maybe.' He went to the window and peered out. Approaching dusk brought lengthened shadows, and an air of gloom seemed to hang over the town now.

'Then it's my fault for placing her in the line of fire,' Tootie mumbled, face grim. 'I wanted to help her but I might have only gotten her killed.'

'It's not your fault, Tootie. She ain't the first young woman to go missing in this town. Two men approached me today, asked me to find their missing daughters. I spent the afternoon looking for leads to them, but came up empty.'

'Reckon that betters her chances of living a bit longer, then.'

He turned back to her. 'Whoever's behind this knows where we are and by taking the girl they want us to know they can get to us whenever they please. I made arrangements with the clerk to change rooms, and paid him well enough to make sure he doesn't give out the number to anyone again.'

'I'm afraid for her, Jim.'

He went to her, wrapped his arms around her and she pressed her head against his chest. 'We'll find her, Tootie.'

'I'm paying that marshal another visit tomorrow. That sonofabitch is going to help find her.'

'Reckon I don't have to tell you to be careful with

97

him. Don't know if he's got a hand in any of this but he's uncooperative as hell.'

'I can take care of myself.'

He hugged her tighter. 'I thought that, too, until I found myself living a pulp novel last night. . . .'

Two hours later he had taken Tootie for a barely touched dinner at the café, then returned to the hotel and moved their belongings to another room two doors down.

He locked the door, unbuckled his gunbelt and tossed it on an ornate chair. This room was a duplicate of the previous one, except the papering was done in blues instead of greens.

Tootie had turned the gaslighting low and stood near the window at the end of the bed, which overlooked a wooden awning and the street below. Her powder-blue nightgown hugged the sleek curves of her body and even a glance at her caused powerful desire to rise in his being. He reckoned her beauty would never stop making his legs go weak.

She turned to him, worry playing on her face, but other emotions as well, ones he wasn't sure how to read.

'I've been thinking a lot lately.'

He gave her a thin smile. 'Lot of that going around.'

'More and more I feel these . . . urges, Jim. I don't know how to explain them, but with the bargirl we helped in Autumn Pass and now this girl . . . I feel. . . .'

'Like you need to be closer to others.'

She nodded. 'Maternal, you might call it. Felt it

start back in Angel Pass, when those kids were disappearing. Not sayin' I want to start a family or anything, least not right now. But I lost my own family when I was a little girl and never got close to anyone . . . till you came along. I'm just sayin' maybe I want more, and down the road. . . .'

His belly cinched as her words trailed off and an uncomfortable surge of emotion flooded him. Lost for words, he remained silent for long moments. Her eyes searched his, making him feel all the more awkward, maybe even a little anxious. 'I ain't a man who deals well with matters of the heart, Tootie. Reckon you know that.'

'If I didn't I'd be the dimmest lantern in the west.' She tried a smile, but it carried an edge of sadness. 'I'm not asking you for anything you can't give me, Jim. And I'm not forcing you to make choices you don't want to make. I'm just telling you . . . I dream about having more, having that stability I never had when I was growing up, and maybe giving it to a child, too.'

He went to the bed, sat on the edge, then spent more time than necessary pulling off his boots.

'I know you want that, Tootie.' He sighed. 'I guess I've known it for a spell now. But I don't know if I can give this up, what we do. . . .'

'I'm not asking you to.'

He gazed at her, face serious. 'Not yet. But you will, one day. Maybe not this year, maybe not even the next. But it'll come because it has to. It's natural for womenfolk.'

A glint of annoyance flashed across her face and

he knew instantly he'd put his foot in it again. But she let it go, turning back to gaze out through the window.

He stood, stripped off his shirt, then tossed it over a bedpost. Frowning, he searched his thoughts for something to blunt his usual tactlessness, but nothing struck him as useful.

He went to her and pulled her into his arms. She yielded to his touch and he knew nothing had ever or would ever compare to the feeling of her body pressed to his.

'I ain't one who's good at saying I'm sorry, Tootie, but. . . .'

She looked up at him, pressed a finger to his lips and said, 'Shhh. I know you can't help yourself sometimes.'

He grunted. 'Why, that almost sounds like sarcasm, Miss del Pelado.'

She didn't answer, merely giggled.

In the ruins of the silver-mine baron's mansion, Alejandro del Pelado sat on a dust- and web-coated sofa in the drawing room. A single kerosene lamp burned low on an insect-infested table beside the chair. A whiskey bottle rested there as well, half empty. Flame light danced across his face in eerie flickering relief, making him look somehow demonic. Glints of flame sparked in his dark eye.

A long time ago. Before he'd become the monster Angela claimed him to be. He recollected good times, weak times, when he had taken her fishing, when he had protected her from other children who despised their mixed breeding. She'd suffered more than he from their taunts. He'd always been able to take care of himself, though now a niggling doubt made him wonder if perhaps she hadn't surpassed him in strength somehow, if in his blind fury and obedience to his doctrine of might he hadn't been left behind.

Foolishness, he assured himself, though the doubt remained. Utter stupidity. Why were such pathetic thoughts invading his mind?

A sudden flash of memory overcame him and he let out a strangled sound of pain. In his mind's eye he saw his father, lying in a pool of blood, saw Deadwood murder his mother. Old feelings of terror and helplessness seized him.

Then anger flooded into his veins, devouring all else. Hannigan. Hannigan had robbed him of the right to avenge his parents' murders; Hannigan had robbed him of his sister, turned her into a despicable bleeding heart. Angela had turned him over to the law in Angel Pass, consigned him to the gallows. If there were one thing he might thank them for, however, it was the bastard emotion that sent blood burning through his veins and hatred raging through his heart: revenge. They had given him that.

And he would thank them personally for it.

Fury sizzled through his lanky frame with the thought. He snatched the whiskey bottle from the table and hurled it at the crumbling fireplace. The bottle shattered with the sound of a gunshot; glass and liquor splashed across the floor.

'Goddamn you!' he yelled, through clenched

teeth. 'Goddamn you both!'

'Alejandro?' came a tentative voice from behind him. He twisted his head to see the two hardcases standing behind him, a measure of fear on both their girlish faces. Fancies, he thought, goddamn fancies, but as deadly a pair as he'd ever had the fortune to hire. Former circus folk, fired for indescribable acts with boys and men, and each other, some of them resulting in murder charges. But skilled in their trade.

Mr Rory came forward, coming up to the chair and gently touching Alejandro's cheek. 'Are you all right, Alejandro?' he asked, voice syrupy.

Alejandro grabbed the man's wrist, squeezed until the smaller man winced with pain and bones crackled. 'Don't ever goddamn touch me, you stupid Nancy.' He released the man's wrist. Mr Rory stepped back as if he'd been bitten by a serpent, then rubbed his wrist.

'He didn't mean nothin' by it,' Mr Ryan said, concern for his partner bleeding onto his face, and a glint of viciousness sparking in his eyes for his employer. 'We were just worried—'

'Don't be.' Alejandro's gaze focused on the fireplace. 'Tomorrow, find Hannigan. Arrange a message. But do not touch the woman. Am I clear?'

'You're clear,' Mr Ryan said.

'Hannigan will change rooms now that he knows we've found out where he's staying. Find out which one he's in. I was told by a lady no longer with us that he enjoys snakes. . . .'

The two hardcases nodded, began backing from the room.

Alejandro smiled. If he knew Hannigan, the manhunter would escape whatever the two arranged, but he preferred it that way. Simply a taunt, a warning. Wear him down, play on his fears.

Another sound came and he looked up to the gypsy standing beside the chair. A sultry smile played on her lips. So smug, that bitch, so completely sure of herself. She'd tried to use her gifts on him a number of times, but his life had no place for a woman, no place for the weak emotions that came with attachments.

'Where have you been?' he asked, voice low, demanding.

She laughed a mocking laugh. It irritated the hell out of him. 'Around. Gal's got things to do.'

'How much money that marshal pay you to service him?' He peered at her, and she suddenly appeared unsure of herself, wary.

'How'd you know?'

He shrugged, smiled thinly. 'You never could stop spreading your legs, could you, Carmella? It's a sickness with you.'

'Some might call it a gift.'

'Really? I suppose. It gives you power over men, does it not?'

She nodded. 'Men are weaklings. They think with their peckers. I see no reason not to take advantage of that.'

His smile widened, the smile of a snake, and her dark eyes narrowed. She took a step back. 'You were instructed not to touch the woman. . . .'

Carmella's face darkened and she wrapped her

arms about herself. 'Those goddamn Nancys told you?'

'I don't suppose your "gifts" would have much power over them, would they? Do you honestly think you could have hidden it from me had you killed her? Do you think you could have used what's between your thighs to convince me it was an accident, that she'd just run into a bullet?'

'It ain't that way, Alejandro—'

He leaped from the chair, fury flashing across his face. His fist snapped up in a short powerful arc and collided with her jaw. She staggered back, dropped to her knees. Blood streamed from her mouth and dripped onto the floor. She uttered a pained gasp, wiped at the blood with the back of her hand.

'Goddamn Christ, Alejandro. . . .' she said, then as she gazed up at him her features froze.

It was the look on his face, he reckoned, the utter contempt for her and absolute rage at her disobedience. Disobedience was a weakness, a fault in character.

His hand went to the Smith & Wesson at his hip. He drew it, pointed it at her head.

'No, please, Alejandro, it won't happen again, I swear. I'll leave her be.'

'Yes, you will.'

He pulled the trigger.

With the dawn Jim Hannigan slipped out of bed, taking care not to awaken Tootie. He stood for a moment watching the gentle rise and fall of her breathing. Early-morning sunlight filtering through the window gilded her face and bare shoulders with an angelic glow. In that moment he had the powerful desire simply to return to the bed, stay with her, forget all about vanished daughters and vengeful killers.

But he had a job to do, and the sooner he tracked down the man who'd tried to murder him the better his chances were of finding the three missing young women alive.

He dressed, then slipped from the room. In the hallway he paused, a peculiar feeling of being watched coming over him. He glanced down the hall, but it was empty. They'd changed rooms, and at such an early hour it seemed unlikely anyone would be lurking about. He went down the hall, making sure no one was around the corner, eventually passing the feeling off as jitters over the decision he'd made during the night, one he'd act on before he checked in with the telegraph office. Still, he stood listening intently for long moments. Nothing, not even the sound of other patrons moving about in their rooms. With a sigh, he threw a last glance behind him, then headed down the stairs and from the hotel.

Mr Rory eased open the door to room 14 and peeked out. He saw an empty hallway and breathed a sigh of relief. Hannigan had damn near caught sight of them, somehow. The man must have been blessed with some sort of second sight. It was rare anyone got a notion of their presence when they didn't want to be seen. Years of practice stealing wallets and handbags at the circuses they'd worked had honed that particular skill.

His partner, Mr Ryan, stood behind him, a square case with a trapdoor on its front resting beside his feet. The case was black and sounds came from inside, sounds that gave Mr Rory the chills: slithers, hisses, muffled thumps. He had news for Alejandro: that Hannigan fella might not care much for snakes but he damn sure had no love for them, either. In fact he hated the goddamned things and Mr Ryan had been forced to gather them from the snake-handler they'd killed in the wee hours of the morning.

'He damn near saw you,' Mr Ryan said.

'Yes, indeed, he damn near did.' Mr Rory eased out into the hallway, pausing to peer around the corner to make sure Hannigan wasn't still waiting there.

'That would have displeased Alejandro.' Mr Ryan, now carrying the black case, came up behind Mr Rory.

'Yes, it most certainly would have. He tolerates no mistakes. A hard man, indeed.'

Mr Ryan nodded. 'As well we know from burying the body of our friend, the dear departed Madam Mystique.'

Mr Rory chuckled. 'I quite hated that woman. She was always trying to entice me into the most atrocious of sins. I suppose we must avenge her at some point, however.'

Mr Ryan frowned at Mr Rory. 'Sins, my pet? Are you not well familiar with such things?'

'Not of the womanly type, Mr Ryan. Her advances displeased and disgusted me.'

'It's a pleasure to see there are still things in this world that do.'

'We'll have to wait until the woman leaves,' Mr Rory said, staring at the door to Hannigan's room. 'Alejandro specifically warned us not to harm the girl. We would not want to suffer Mystique's fate.'

Mr Ryan nodded, smiling. 'It's a shame such a handsome man has to die.'

'Yes, a shame, indeed, but who may stay the hand of fate?'

'When by its hand does the river of life abate. . . .'

Mr Rory giggled. 'In the meantime, might we not entertain ourselves? We have the room we rented. . . .'

'My sentiments exactly. . . .' Mr Ryan touched his partner's cheek.

Tootie opened her eyes and sat up the minute Jim Hannigan left the room. She pulled the covers over her bosom and glanced out through the sun-glazed window. Its curtains billowed with the warm breeze that came through the two-inch opening; she felt it caress her skin like the whisper of his fingertips and a soft smile came to her lips.

The smile faded quickly, though, when she thought of their conversation last night. She had seen fear in his eyes, but far less resistance than she might have expected. That was the reason she hadn't taken him to task for his callous remark about womenfolk, because his true feelings had shown through and he had come to them on his own, even before she had brought it up. She had wondered at times, perhaps out of her own insecurity, whether their relationship had the solid ground necessary to sustain it, whether perhaps now that she had lain with him he no longer felt a need to carry things further.

She'd been thinking about carrying it further herself for ages, since Angel Pass, when she'd felt the first stirrings of that maternal instinct. She realized a stable life with him wasn't in the cards for the immediate future, of course, but she had to know from him that someday it would be, that she meant a future, not simply the comfort of a warm body when he needed it.

She reckoned she knew better, knew it wasn't that way, but a woman needed something more, something . . . *committed.*

She would never ask him to quit this life of manhunting. And she would stay by his side as long as he wanted to continue it, though she had to admit the notion of a small ranch somewhere and raising a family appealed to her more and more as days went on. Yet danger ran in her own blood as well and she needed to work that out before giving serious thought to settling down.

She climbed out of bed and dressed, her mind turning to matters of the moment. Druella Bradly was likely alive for the time being, possibly hidden away with the two other young women who'd gone missing. She didn't know how long that situation would hold but she knew she had to find a lead to them before they permanently vanished into the West.

The vanishings with this case tied in with whoever had lured Hannigan to Widow's Pass. She felt certain of it.

No, not whoever. *Him.* He was alive, and she had to face that fact. Everything pointed to Alejandro, though she hadn't told Hannigan her suspicions. He would only want to protect her, leave her out of things, and she was stronger than that. She had spent months dealing with the fact that her brother had become a monster. She had thought him dead, hanged, but the moment she encountered the gypsy she had feared a link to him. Mystique would have no compelling reason to seek vengeance on her own.

She shivered and a deep sadness washed through her. She hated the fact that life made a body face pain that there was no call to face. She hoped she would be strong enough when the time came to do whatever proved necessary to stop him from hurting Hannigan or Druella, to make certain he never got the chance to harm anyone ever again.

After leaving the hotel, she stopped at the café for a quick breakfast before going to confront the marshal. Hannigan might not be certain the man was involved in anything untoward but she sure as hell pegged him as crooked. It was intuition more than anything else, she supposed, but she had relied on that for most of her young life and rarely did it steer her wrong.

On her way to the marshal's office her mind churned with thoughts of Druella and Alejandro, Jim

Hannigan and the future. She forced herself to focus, stay alert. After the attempt on her life yesterday, which she had neglected to tell Hannigan about, she could not afford a lapse in attention.

She scanned the rooftops for any sign of a sniper. She saw no one. Her attention shifted to the street and early risers milling about, looking not only for the two hardcases and the gypsy, but any hint of suspicious intent on a stranger's face. She saw nothing but sleepy eyes and folks intent on their own destinations.

A few moments later she entered the marshal's office to find the lawdog shaving over a porcelain basin atop a small table. He was gazing into a wall mirror and wore an undershirt. A small towel was draped about his neck.

His gaze flicked to her as she shut the door. 'Forgive me if I don't wish you "good morning",' he said. He dropped the straight razor onto the table, then toweled the remaining lather from his face.

'Reckon you got a notion why I'm here.' The sight of the man sent a surge of anger through her she hadn't expected. The thought of him doing nothing for Druella had simmered in her belly and was boiling over now.

'No, I'm afraid I do not, Miss del Pelado. Why, pray tell, would you be blessing me with your presence at this ungodly hour?' He tossed the towel to the table, then plucked his shirt from a wall hook and shrugged into it.

'Druella Bradly. I got a notion you know where she is.' Tootie stepped deeper into the office, her gaze

110

remaining locked on Hicks. He showed no surprise at her accusation and in her mind that confirmed his involvement in this case.

The marshal grabbed his gunbelt from the back of a chair and strapped it on. 'How the hell would I know where she is? I recollect that you said you had custody of her at your hotel.'

Tootie came closer to him, her mahogany eyes hard, unwavering. 'When I got back to my room yesterday she was gone, but I figure you already knew that, didn't you?'

'I'm sure you're mistaken, miss. That girl likely ran off on her own, back to her pa, I figure. She never was any good and couldn't do without his special lovin'—'

Tootie buried a foot in his crotch. She couldn't stop herself. Rage and disgust overcame her and before she knew it the marshal was on his knees, gasping.

'You think Jim Hannigan's hell on hoofs, Marshal, you just go ahead and say something else stupid to my face.'

He looked up at her, eyes watery but laced with fury. He grasped his southern parts and spittle gathered at the corners of his mouth. 'You and your partner get the hell out of my town . . . or I swear I'll hang you both.'

Tootie didn't flinch. 'Alejandro del Pelado, Marshal. That name ring a bell? Have you seen my brother?'

Shock flashed across his face, quickly hidden, but not quickly enough. Tootie knew she had him. He was involved in the case and her brother *was* alive. Her belly sank, though she had expected the revelation.

The marshal's expression turned back to fury and pain. 'Don't know what the hell you're talking about.' His words came without a lot of conviction.

'Oh, I reckon you do. And I reckon you just got yourself invited to a necktie party of your own ... unless you tell me where he has Druella Bradly and the two other girls who went missing.' Her hand slipped into her skirt pocket and she brought out the derringer. She leveled it on the lawdog's forehead. 'Or maybe I'll just save the law the trouble and put a bullet between your eyes.' At that moment she damn well might have pulled the trigger. It was all she could do not to.

The marshal's eyes narrowed to a glare. 'Go to hell, you stupid bitch. You won't find them and you won't find *him*. But he'll find you when the time comes.'

She gave him a grim smile. 'The gloves are off now, aren't they, Marshal? You've been helping him all along.'

The move caught her by surprise. One moment she was finishing her sentence and considering shooting him just for the satisfaction of it, then next his hand snapped out and caught her ankle. She had misjudged him; he'd recovered faster than she expected and anger had prevented her from picking up on anything that might have betrayed his intent.

He yanked, hard, and she went backwards. She slammed into the floor on her back. The impact took her breath away and the derringer flew from her grip. It skipped across the floor and came to a stop under the desk.

The marshal was on her before she could even think about moving. He jammed a gun into her face and the look on his features told her the slightest move on her part would result in a bullet punching into her brain.

'Get up, Miss del Pelado,' he ordered, then backed off her.

She struggled to her feet, legs shaky.

'Turn around,' he said, and she complied. 'You wanted to know where that girl went to, well, now I'll take you to her. I reckon it'll give you and your brother a chance to catch up on old times. . . .'

That was the last she heard. His gun butt crashed into the back of her skull. She had heard the swish of his clothing, tried to jerk her head sideways, but the blow came too fast. She hit the floor face first. Through bleary eyes she saw boots pause before her, then blackness swallowed her senses.

CHAPTER EIGHT

If Jim Hannigan had ever felt as nervous as he did at this moment, he couldn't remember it. After pausing outside the little shop, he stared at the gilt lettering that arced across the plate-glass window: HANNITY'S JEWELERS. Below, in smaller lettering: Importers of Fine Jewels Since 1849.

He'd never given any thought to marriage before meeting Tootie. He'd figured that particular institution to be the domain of henpecked church fellas and farmers who needed help around the ranch. Matrimony wasn't for the manhunter, a fella who spent his life alone on the trail. But she had changed his way of thinking. Over the past year she had unearthed feelings in him he would never have believed possible, about himself, about the choices one had in life, about commitment.

A man didn't have to spend his life alone; he chose that option himself. He isolated himself based on his own experience and fear and it was nearly always the wrong direction. Being with a woman brought its share of problems, risks and aggravations, but he could no longer imagine his life without her. And the least he could do was provide her the security of knowing she meant more than just a body to fill the empty nights on the trail.

It was now or never, Hannigan. If you stand outside the shop much longer you'll lose your nerve.

He cast a quick look behind him, at the early-morning townsfolk heading to cafés or various shops. A buckboard rattled past. He drew a deep breath, steadied himself and went to the shop door. He noticed his palm was damp as he gripped the handle. By the look of his reflection in the door window, anyone might have figured he was walking to the gallows instead of purchasing a ring.

As he entered the shop, a bell above the door jangled. A man behind a display counter looked up, gave him the once-over and registered mild disapproval.

Hannigan walked to the counter. Smiling a small smile, he tossed a wad of greenbacks onto the glass top. The clerk's expression instantly shifted to eager anticipation.

'Why, how may I help you this fine morning, my good man?' The clerk beamed now, any snobbery washed away by the prospect of a sale. He was a small man, with graying temples and a hooked nose with nostrils that could have used a shearing.

'I'm looking for. . . .' he hesitated, the words locking in his throat.

'An engagement ring,' the clerk answered for him, nodding.

'How'd you—'

'Every fella who comes in lookin' to buy an

engagement ring has that attending-his-own-hangin' expression on his face. Been in this business enough years to recognize the look.'

Hannigan's smile widened with a measure of relief at not having to say the words. 'Reckon I want the best you have.'

'Of course.' The man peered beneath the counter, examining the many displays of rings. They all looked pretty much the same to Hannigan. He'd never been much for sparkly things.

The clerk selected a ring, polished it on a lapel of his boiled shirt, then passed it to Hannigan. Hannigan noticed his hand shaking as he took the ring and examined it. The stone, bigger than any he'd ever seen, glittered.

'This one's a bit much, I reckon. She's a simple gal. Rock this size might scare her away.'

The clerk grinned. 'Well, I always try to sell that one first. It's our most expensive. What size did you say her ring finger was?'

Hannigan handed the ring back to the clerk. 'Size? They come in sizes?'

The clerk gave him a cocky expression. 'Why, of course. Greta!' he yelled, and a young woman scurried out from the back room.

'Yes, Mr Hannity?' she said.

'Show the gentleman your hand.'

'My hand?' She looked puzzled.

'Yes, yes, your hand.' The shop-owner grabbed her hand and placed it on the counter top, fingers splayed. 'This about the size of your intended's?'

Hannigan peered at the girl's hand. Her fingers

looked nearly the same size as Tootie's, but he could-
n't be positive. 'I reckon that's about right.'

'Thank you, Greta.' The man released the girl and
she scooted into the back room. 'Well, if it's wrong,
you can always come back with her and have it sized.'
He peered beneath the counter again, selected a
more modest but elegant ring. Hannigan shifted
feet. Sweat trickled from beneath his arms and down
his sides.

'Ah, this one!' The clerk brought out the ring and
passed it to Hannigan.

He much preferred the looks of this one. Smaller,
but it somehow matched the woman for whom it was
intended. 'This'll do,' he said. Damn, he felt
awkward as hell and a hitch rode his voice that he
didn't appreciate.

The clerk nodded, took back the ring and put it in
a velvet case. Fifteen minutes later Hannigan was
back on the boardwalk, shaking like he'd jumped
into an ice-cold pond, the ring tucked safely in a
pocket. It dawned on him that picking out a ring was
the easy part. Asking her . . . well, that would have to
come later. He needed to tie up this case first and
determine whether they were truly dealing with a
man he'd thought dead for six months.

He went to the telegraph office and entered to
find the clerk just writing out an incoming message.
The clerk finished scrawling on a slip, looked up,
recognizing him.

'Mr Hannigan, something came for you.' He rifled
through a stack of yellow papers, selected one, then
came over to Hannigan and handed it to him.

Hannigan nodded his thanks and left the office. Pausing on the boardwalk, he took a deep breath then peered at the slip:

MARSHAL WENTWORTH DECEASED STOP RAJAS VAGO ESCAPED STOP WHEREABOUTS UNKNOWN STOP

'Christ,' he mumbled, his worst fears confirmed. Now he knew why he'd been drawn to Widow's Pass: Alejandro del Pelado had somehow escaped his fate and wanted revenge.

He crumpled the telegram and stuffed it into a pocket. How the hell was he going to tell Tootie her brother had not died in Angel Pass six months ago as scheduled? He wished he didn't have to, but he couldn't hide it from her now that he knew for certain. She would never forgive him if he did.

He sighed, his heart heavy as he stepped off the boardwalk and walked towards the hotel.

An incessant banging in her skull brought Tootie back to awareness. Dull at first, distant, it grew more acute by the moment, until she could no longer ignore it and forced her eyes to open.

She discovered herself in a root-cellar, her back pressed against a damp stone wall, moist earth at her feet. The air smelled of must and decay. Ropes bound her wrists and ankles.

She twisted her head upon hearing a sound beside her; a mistake, because it made her skull feel like someone had struck it with a hammer. Her vision blurred with the pain. She drew a deep breath, pressed her eyes shut again, then opened them and waited until her sight focused and the pounding in her head settled into a throbbing drum.

Beside her sat three young women, Druella Bradly and two others who she assumed belonged to the men who'd wanted to hire Hannigan. All were bound and gagged. She was bound, though whoever had brought her here had neglected a gag.

'Angela. . . .' A voice drifted from the shadows across the chamber and her belly sank. She recognized that voice. She lifted her head, peered into those shadows. A man stepped forward and she couldn't suppress a small gasp.

Light from a low-turned lantern on a small table to the right of her fell across his bearded face like sulfur flame shining on the twisted visage of a demon from hell. He appeared much more haggard than when she last saw him, a little over six months ago, in Angel Pass. The months on the run had worn on him and the insane, detached look in his eye appeared stronger than ever.

'Alejandro. . . .' She was unable to keep the tremor from her voice.

He stepped closer. 'Surprised to see me?'

'I wish I could say yes, but I suspected it was you the moment that gypsy tried to kill me. How did you escape the hangman's noose?'

He peered at her, the detached look strengthened. 'Huh, somehow I expected more . . . *relief* in your voice.'

'I came to terms with your death months ago, Alejandro. Reckon any expression of relief now

119

would be a sign of weakness on my part.'

He smiled. '*Touché.* Our dear Mystique outlived her usefulness, incidentally. She won't be troubling you again.'

Tootie's eyes narrowed, but she felt no regret over the disclosure. 'You killed her?'

He ignored the question. His head lowered, came back up a moment later. 'I made you an offer six months ago, Angela. Join me. Be strong. We can have a family again, everything we ever wanted.'

'At the expense of these women?' she said, spite in her tone. 'At the expense of Jim Hannigan's life?'

'Casualties of war, Angela. They are weak human beings. They aren't like us. We're strong, survivors.'

'You're still a monster, Alejandro. And a disgrace to the del Pelado name.'

He nodded, face grim, lips tight. 'I expected as much from you. Whatever ingrained that spark of decency in you, I curse it. It's done you no good.'

He turned, gripped the ladder beneath the trap-door, which was open.

'What are you going to do with us?' she asked, knowing the answer full well.

He looked back to her. 'Your decision didn't affect only yourself, Angela. It's time you learn everything has consequences. You consigned these young women to death the moment you refused my offer.'

He went up the ladder, not looking back again. She watched him climb, saw the door close behind him.

She hadn't known how she would react upon seeing him again, but all she felt was a strange deadness inside, then a sudden panic that her brother would go after Hannigan first, before killing her and the other women.

She struggled furiously against her ropes, but had no luck loosening them, only skinning flesh from her wrists, which stung and bled.

She'd never break free in time to stop her brother and a great dread washed through her with the thought. She whispered a prayer that Hannigan would somehow escape Alejandro and find this place, wherever it was.

Alejandro del Pelado strode into the mansion's drawing room, his heart leaden. He had known she would never join him but he'd coddled a guttering wish, the tiniest of hopes, that she'd be strong, change her mind. But she was too far gone. Hannigan had corrupted her. Another sin for which the manhunter would atone with his life.

Another man stood in the parlor, peering out through the fractured bay windows. He turned when Alejandro entered.

'Thank you for bringing her to me, Hicks,' Alejandro said.

The lawdog frowned, face dark. 'She knew everything, somehow. Figured I had no other choice.'

Alejandro nodded. 'Reckon you did not. Those two idiot Nancys . . . I sent them to deliver a warning to Hannigan. I have no doubt he'll escape it. Bring him here when he does. Now that I have Angela it's time to end this.'

A startled look crossed the marshal's face as he

turned towards Alejandro. 'How the hell do I do that? He won't be as easy to get the jump on as a girl. That guy's reputation isn't any pulp tale.'

Alejandro nodded, his eyelid fluttering. 'Tell him you saw Mr Rory and Mr Ryan kidnap Angela and that you followed them here. Come with him. I'll be waiting.'

The marshal sighed, but gave a curt nod. 'You sure about that? He's one dangerous sonofabitch—'

'Just do it.' Alejandro went to the windows and stared past the man, out into the daylight. 'And Hicks. . . .'

'Yeah?'

'Set the fire charges the way I showed you at the corners of this room before you leave.'

The marshal peered at him as if he'd lost his mind but after a moment turned and left the room.

Jim Hannigan returned to his hotel room a little past ten in the morning. He'd sifted through ways in his mind to tell Tootie her brother was still alive and decided plain and direct was the best course. He owed her the truth, though he dreaded the pain it would cause her.

No one should have to face the death of a loved one twice, even if that loved one had gone bad.

Lead in his heart, he made his way down the hall, paused before the door to their room and took a deep breath. After fishing the key from his pocket, he gripped the handle, stopped, a quiver of warning riding his nerves. The door was unlocked. Had Tootie forgotten to lock it when she left? Or had the gypsy or the two hardcases discovered the new room and set a trap?

He slipped the key back into his pocket, then eased the handle around. He drew his Peacemaker, stepped to the side, then threw open the door.

No shots came from within, no sound. He whirled, bending low, Peacemaker out-thrust before him. He arced the weapon left, then right, but the room was empty.

He blew out a relieved breath, returned the Peacemaker to its holster, then stepped into the room. Maybe Tootie, distracted over the Bradly girl, *had* simply forgotten to lock it.

With his next step forward, he froze. His foot had encountered something giving. He looked down, discovering a thin string had been stretched two inches above the floor and went from the bureau to a chair. The line, nearly invisible, hadn't broken and one would have had to have been purposely looking for it to have had a chance of spotting it in time to avoid snapping it. He'd gotten lucky. A backward glance showed him the thread angled around the bureau leg and traveled along the wall beside the door.

Tensing, he eased back his foot, hoping he hadn't stretched the string enough to trigger whatever it was attached to.

A click sounded as the string went taut. With a sinking dread, he knew whoever had set the trap had built in a safeguard in case the string wasn't broken. Once pulled, either easing back or breaking it completely was enough to activate the mechanism to which it was attached.

He whirled, gaze sweeping upwards to the source of the click.

Secured above the door was a box, on which a flap had sprung open.

Hannigan's arm jerked up in an effort to deflect the rain of serpents that suddenly tumbled from the box. In nearly the same move he tried to jump backwards, but couldn't avoid all the writhing creatures.

'Jesus!' he yelled, at least twenty snakes of varying sizes falling over his arm and shoulder. Most rebounded to the floor. A wave of chills washing through him, he flailed his arm in a panic, hurling loose a coiling snake. The serpent ricocheted from the wall and hit the floor, instantly hissing and angling forward.

He froze, recognizing at least two of the species as deadly and realizing he was damned lucky he hadn't been bitten.

Agitated by the fall, the serpents slithered toward him. Tongues flicking, hissing, they writhed over one another. A rattler, tail buzzing, coiled, reared to strike, its angular head inches from his boot-covered shin.

He jerked from his spell, reacting without thought. His foot snapped out, caught the thing square on the head and sent it flying backward. It bounced from a wall, unharmed, resumed its forward course.

Other snakes, some glistening black, some multi-ringed, all poisonous, slithered closer. He backed up, sweat springing out on his forehead. There were too many. He could shoot some, but not enough, and they blocked his path to the door.

Mind racing, he threw a glance behind him, his gaze locking the position of the window. He was on the second story and a leap would risk a broken arm or leg, but if he recollected right a wooden awning lay below, directly above the first floor. He looked forward again. The snakes slithered closer.

He had no choice. He couldn't jump over them and chance being bitten.

A black serpent's tongue flickered inches from his boot toe.

A surge of revulsion rushing through him, he whirled, leaping to the window. He grabbed it, tried to thrust it up so he could climb out.

The window wouldn't budge. A glance told him someone had pounded nails into the base, sealing it shut.

Closer.

Behind him, hissing crescendoed. The sound of their bodies sliding across the floor made him shudder.

He backed away from the window a step, crossed his forearms before his face, then hurtled himself forward. He slammed full force into the window. Glass and wooden cross-strips exploded about him as he crashed through.

Shards lacerated the air, some slicing his hands and arms, but thankfully missing his face. Legs peddling, he went down, crashed into the awning and bounced. The awning broke his fall some but he still slammed hard onto the hard-packed street. He rolled instantly to absorb some of the shock. After coming to a stop, bruised and scraped, he remained still a moment, breath beating out, then sat up. He felt like he'd been kicked by a mule, but nothing seemed to be broken.

He climbed to his feet, body aching, legs shaking, but thankful to be away from the snakes. He'd been lucky this time. He peered up at his room window, suppressed a shudder.

A number of passers-by stared at him, shock on their faces. He shrugged, gave them a sheepish grin, then went back into the hotel, gait unsteady, and located the clerk. He told him about the snakes in the room and the man informed him he'd heard the local snake handler had been murdered the previous night, but he would find someone else to trap the things immediately. Hannigan had no desire to return to the room anytime soon.

He left the hotel, absently patting the pocket in which he'd tucked the ring, to make sure it was still there.

'Mr Hannigan?' a voice came from the boardwalk behind him. He turned.

'Marshal. . . .'

'What the hell happened?' The marshal's gaze went to the pieces of glass and board littering the street. 'A witness said a fella came through the hotel window and landed in the street.'

'Reckon that'd be me. Someone left me an unpleasant surprise in my room. I had a limited choice of exits.'

The marshal nodded, looked up at the broken

window then back to Hannigan. 'You could have been killed. . . .'

Hannigan cocked an eyebrow, unable to read the man's tone. 'Reckon that was the intent.'

The lawdog looked at the ground, lips pursed, then up again. 'Seems I owe you an apology, Mr Hannigan. I misjudged you. Figure maybe it would be better if we worked together than at odds.'

Suspicion crawled through in Hannigan's mind. 'You suddenly get religion or is there a reason behind your change of heart?'

The marshal nodded, face sincere, though Hannigan wondered whether it was an act. 'Saw two men, two Nancy hardcases, take your lady friend.'

'What?' Hannigan's belly plunged. He grabbed the marshal and jerked him close. 'What the hell are you talking about, Hicks?'

The marshal's expression didn't change. 'Easy now, Hannigan. I'm in a cordial mood, but it won't last long if you don't get your hands offa me.'

Hannigan studied the man's face, then released him, worry over Tootie clouding his judgment for a moment. 'What happened.'

'They waylaid her, caught her coming out of the café. Figured I could try stopping them but then you wouldn't know who sent them after her. So I followed them. I know where they are and figured you'd want to go after them with me.'

'You best not be lying, Marshal. I ain't in the frame of mind to be forgiving.'

Hicks shrugged. 'I trailed them out to the old silver-mine mansion. They met another fella there.'

'What did this fella look like?'

'Saw him through the window, but I could tell he had a beard and an eyepatch.'

'Alejandro. . . .' muttered Hannigan.

'Who?' the marshal asked.

'Someone from the past, Marshal. A monster.'

'I got two horses already dressed for the ball. Do we ride out there after those men?'

'We do.' Hannigan didn't trust the lawdog but for now he had no other options. Hicks would bear watching and the moment the marshal misstepped Hannigan would put a bullet between his eyes. Alejandro del Pelado, guessing the snake trap would fail, had issued an invitation by taking Tootie. Jim Hannigan was all too happy to accept.

CHAPTER NINE

Fifteen minutes later Jim Hannigan and Marshal Hicks reined to a halt in front of the silver-mine baron's mansion. Hannigan dismounted first, keeping a close eye on Hicks as the lawman climbed from his horse.

Hannigan's attention focused on the house. 'You sure they're inside? I searched this place once already and came up empty.'

The lawdog nodded. 'I'm sure. The girl was unconscious, but alive.'

Hannigan glanced at the man. The marshal would have made a hell of a poker-player, he decided. He couldn't tell whether Hicks were lying.

'I'll scout the outside.' Hannigan pulled his Peacemaker from its holster. 'I want to make sure those two hardcases aren't waiting to ambush us.'

The marshal's expression didn't change. 'I'll keep an eye on the front, make sure no one comes out.'

Hannigan slipped away, suspicious of the lawman, but for the moment more concerned that Tootie might be in danger. He scouted the perimeter of the house, but no one was in sight. The mansion appeared as deserted as it had the previous day.

He came back around the front, eased up the stairs then to the bay windows. When he gazed inside, his heart skipped a beat. A man sat in a wing-backed chair, a man whom, just a few days ago, he had thought dead, courtesy of a hangman's noose. Alejandro del Pelado. Tootie's brother. Alive.

'Christ. . . .' Hannigan mumbled. The man appeared oblivious to the manhunter's presence; he simply stared straight ahead. Hannigan saw no sign of Tootie.

His hand tightened on the grip of his gun. He backed away from the window, glanced over at the marshal, who now stood at the bottom of the steps.

'Well, you weren't lyin' 'bout him being in there.'

Hicks nodded, slipping up the stairs. 'We go in?'

Hannigan nodded. 'We go in.'

The manhunter went to the door, pushed it open. His gun swung left, then right, in case the hardcases were waiting in the vestibule to ambush them.

The vestibule was empty.

He moved toward the drawing room, gun leveling on the big chair as he entered. Alejandro had not moved. He looked up as Hannigan came around the chair and stopped in front of him.

'I've been waiting for you, Mr Hannigan. I'm not certain how you escaped my little reception at the train tracks, but I half-expected it. That's why I wore the mask, besides my penchant for melodrama. I reckon killing you face to face will be much more pleasing, however.'

'Where the hell is she?' Hannigan gestured with

the Peacemaker, in no mood for theatrics or insanity. And looking into the bearded man's dark eye it was plain to see Alejandro del Pelado had indeed lost his grip on reality.

'Angela? She's here. She'll be buried with the house along with you, don't worry.'

A skritching sound came from behind Hannigan and he froze, ice pooling in his belly. The sight of the man before him had made him sloppy. He looked up to see Hicks holding a gun on him.

'Don't do anything stupid, Mr Hannigan.' Hicks finger shook ever so slightly on the trigger, which made him more dangerous than a calm, practiced gunfighter.

Alejandro del Pelado arose from his chair and took Hannigan's gun. The bearded man leveled it on the manhunter, smiled.

'What was the one thing that would make you let your guard down, Mr Hannigan? I asked myself. Of course, the answer was painfully obvious – any danger to that wayward sister of mine.'

'We should just kill him before he has a chance to escape again.' Hicks gestured with his gun. Alejandro gazed at him, shook his head.

'No, Marshal, I have something else in mind for Mr Hannigan. I've waited a long time for this. I don't plan to have the moment spoiled by anything as mundane as a quick death.'

'But—'

'You may leave now, Marshal Hicks. I thank you for your service. Please activate the charges on the way out.'

131

'How will you get out?' Puzzlement crossed the marshal's features.

Alejandro del Pelado smiled, a peculiar vacant expression, but didn't answer.

The lawman peered at him another moment, as if judging the man hopelessly insane, then went in turn to each side of the drawing room entrance and turned a small dial on a mechanism attached to two jars of amber liquid resting on the floor. Hannigan studied the jars, noting the coils leading to a wick thrust into each. The small clocks attached to both jars now ticked away seconds.

The marshal backed from the room, leaving Hannigan with Alejandro.

'What the hell are those?'

Alejandro smiled. 'An associate I called upon recently taught me the fine art of murder from a distance. The timers, when they stop in a few seconds, will ignite the jars' contents.'

'This whole place. . . .'

'Will go up in flames in a heartbeat, I would guess, taking you and my sister with it. It adds to the drama, don't you think? So much more fitting than being run over by a train; I can see that now.'

'You figurin' on dyin' with me?' Hannigan's gaze remained locked with Alejandro's. Only a couple feet stood between him and the man, though the gun was aimed directly at his belly. Any sudden move chanced a bullet through the gut.

Without a word, Alejandro started to lower the gun and Hannigan instantly saw his plan: The man intended to cripple him, leave him behind to burn and be buried under tons of debris.

As if in response, a double *whoosh* sounded from the doorway as the clocks hit zero and set off the fire-bomb charges. Flames exploded over the floor and half-way up the wall.

Alejandro smiled as the flames devoured the dried wood like kindling. Despite the risk, Hannigan acted. He saw no other choice. He twisted, at the same time hurtling forward, hands grabbing for the Peacemaker in Alejandro's grip.

A shot blasted. A bullet tore a gory furrow across Hannigan's left side. It bled liberally but the wound was superficial.

He grabbed the Peacemaker, jerked. Another shot came, but the bullet went up, buried itself in the ceiling; plaster rained.

Alejandro kicked at Hannigan's shins, wrenched at the gun. He was powerful; Hannigan had all he could do to keep a grip on the weapon.

Alejandro whirled Hannigan around, nearly dislodging the Peacemaker. Hannigan managed to hang on, barely. He countered with kicks of his own at the circus man's knees, but Alejandro somehow sidestepped each.

At the room entrance flame whisked over old papering, clawed at the ceiling. Black smoke billowed out, swirling through the room. It stung his eyes, choked his lungs. Beams began to creak, groan, as if the house were a living creature in the throes of death.

'Why won't you just die?' yelled Alejandro through gritted teeth.

Sweat poured from Hannigan's brow and from under his arms. His grip was faltering on the gun. The heat, nearly unbearable now, sapped his strength and smoke strangled his breathing.

Alejandro let out a roar and made a desperate attempt to wrench the gun loose. He was strong but the heat and smoke were affecting his endurance as well.

Hannigan, summoning the strength he had left, flung the man around. Alejandro stumbled, lost his hold on the gun, but managed to somehow jerk the trigger as his hands came loose. The Peacemaker discharged, flew from Hannigan's grip and hit the floor. It spun away, coming to a stop half a dozen feet from the wing-backed chair.

Alejandro quickly regained his balance and hurled himself at Hannigan. Insane light danced in the man's eye, and spittle gathered at the corners of his mouth.

Hannigan countered with an uppercut as the man lunged. It took Alejandro under the jaw, nearly lifting him off the floor.

He staggered, blood dribbling from his lips.

Hannigan, shaking, weakness flooding his legs, hit him again. This time the circus man collapsed to his knees, gasping, coughing.

Heat started to blister Hannigan's skin. He knew there wasn't much time before the entire place crashed down on them, if the smoke and heat didn't kill them first.

Alejandro looked up at the manhunter, his face crimson, blistering, his eye half-closed.

'Why won't you just . . . die. . . .' He fell forward, slamming face first into the floor. His breath rasped, but he didn't move. Hannigan yanked Alejandro's gun from its holster and flung it out through a paneless window.

After, he ran to his own gun, grabbed it, nearly dropped it again because it had become red-hot. He fumbled it into his holster, then lunged from the room, guessing there was only one place Alejandro would be keeping Tootie and the other girls – the root-cellar he hadn't been able to open. If he were wrong, they would all die in this house.

Staggering now, Hannigan stumbled into the pantry, whose door hung open. He went to the trap-door, grabbed the metal ring and yanked. The door came up this time and he hurled it aside with a crash.

He peered into the hole, saw the ladder and a glow coming from beneath. Sheer will driving him, he took the rungs in clumsy bounds, his strength nearly exhausted. He gave no thought to caution and had the two hardcases been hiding down there he might have died in that instant. But they weren't.

'Jim!' yelled Tootie. She had half-freed herself from her bonds; blood ran along her wrists and pieces of rope showed in her teeth.

He went to her, grabbed the knife from his boot sheath and sliced the ropes at her ankles and wrists. After, he jumped to the other women and cut them loose. Tootie got to her feet, wobbling, while he helped the other girls up. The young women pulled out their gags.

'We have to get out of here fast,' he said, between

gasps. 'The whole place is going to come down. Alejandro set it afire.'

Tootie nodded, guiding the other women toward the ladder. 'Is he. . . ?'

'He's alive for the moment.'

Hannigan herded the girls up the ladder. Tootie scrambled up after them and he went up last. Tootie grabbed his hand and heaved as he faltered near the top, getting him out of the trapdoor, then she pulled him along.

They made their way down the hall to the vestibule. Flame had nearly blocked their paths. Tongues lashed at the walls and across the floor, leaving only a small pathway. Even so, skirts had to be gathered for risk of catching fire. Huge plumes of black smoke gouted from the drawing room.

A huge crash sounded as a beam crashed down with a flurry of stinging sparks and a blast of black smoke. A wave of flame shot across the drawing room entrance.

'Alejandro,' Tootie whispered, shock on her features.

'He's gone, Tootie.' Hannigan urged her forward before they all met the same fate.

They came out onto the porch, coughing, staggering. The house groaned and creaked and more beams came crashing down within.

They hurried down the steps and over to the horse on which Hannigan had ridden in, then watched as flames ripped through windows and finally stabbed through the mansion roof. Like a great dying beast the building uttered one last enormous moan and the roof collapsed. Great clouds of smoke billowed into the sky and flames leaped into the air. From within came explosions and crashes as the house vanished in an inferno.

Within the crumbling remains of the mansion, Alejandro del Pelado looked up and saw Jim Hannigan rush from the room. He smiled, a thin laugh trembling from his lips. Hannigan's weakness: Angela. Predictable, as always. That was what separated him from the manhunter. He would have sacrificed his sister in favor of the kill. Now the manhunter had missed his chance to destroy for good the man who'd come seeking revenge. Alejandro would make sure that came back to haunt Hannigan in the few days the sonofabitch had left.

Alejandro began to crawl, fingers bleeding as they gouged into the floor. His lungs burned and his face had blistered, blackened. Little strength remained in his body and his arms trembled as he dragged himself towards a side window. A beam collapsed near the drawing room entrance. *Not much time . . .* he thought. *Not much . . . time. . . .*

His consciousness wavered, the blackness of billowing smoke mingling with the ebony clouds drifting through his mind. His head hit the floor, the pain of contact jolting him back to awareness.

The window. A few feet away. He grunted, summoning the last of his strength to reach it. At the wall he struggled to pull himself up to the window. The pane had long ago fallen out and if he could just get to the fresh air, pull himself through. . . .

Strength. He was the strong one, the one who had always survived, always *would* survive.

His grip slipped, and he knew he could not make it, could not reach the outside. He slumped, but something grabbed his arm from the outside, jerked. Upward his body came and he saw a face through tear- and smoke-clouded eyes.

'Hicks. . . .' he whispered.

'Goddammit, Alejandro, I told you just to shoot him.'

Alejandro laughed, the sound, fluttery, half-insane. Marshal Hicks yanked him the rest of the way through the window, then clamped an arm around Alejandro's shoulders and pulled him away from the blazing mansion.

A day later, Jim Hannigan had bandaged the small wound in his side and returned the two young women to their fathers, both of whom had been overcome with emotion and gratitude. He and Tootie had relocated to a different hotel, Hannigan having no desire to return to the previous hostelry, despite the fact the snakes had all been collected. Tootie found some sort of peculiar humor in the notion of a man who hunted down dangerous criminals and often slept on the trail being afraid of snakes. She'd been ribbing him about it most of the morning, but he reckoned that helped take her mind off the death of her brother. For the moment she was handling it with poise and self-control, but he knew it would hit her all at once at some point and if she fell he would be there to catch her.

Despite an intensive search, he'd turned up no sign of the two hardcases or Marshal Hicks. He'd organize a search for them at some later point, but assumed with Alejandro gone they had pulled stakes rather than risk a hangman's noose.

That left one piece of unfinished business.

Hannigan reined up before the ramshackle homestead of Marcus Bradly. The noon-day sun blazed, making him sweat. His heart beat a mite faster with the thought of the grim task confronting him. The decision had not come lightly, but after questioning Druella earlier this morning, he'd found her hatred for her father absolute. Despite horrendous pain in her eyes, she had detailed every perverted act and abuse the man had forced upon her, and it fell in line perfectly with a number of things Hannigan had discovered upon going through dodgers and the previous marshal's papers at the Hick's office.

Marcus Bradly was a monster. His crimes went beyond the deflowering and defiling of his daughter, but those crimes had been either neatly hidden or ignored by Hicks and the marshal before him. In the final tally, Bradly might have been in the same category as Alejandro del Pelado, just more stupid and lazy.

He dismounted, guided his horse beneath a sturdy cottonwood. He pulled a rope with a noose from his saddle and slung it over a high branch, so it dangled a few feet above the saddle.

He wiped a line of sweat from his brow, steeled himself, then went to the door of the homestead. He pounded a fist against the old wood, then stepped back a couple inches, readying himself. A moment

139

later, Marcus Bradly, obviously half-drunk, filled the doorway. Hannigan hit him. Bradly flew backwards and landed on the floor flat on his back.

Hannigan stepped into the house and drew his Peacemaker, aiming it at Bradly.

'Get the hell up,' Hannigan said.

Bradly peered up at him, bleary-eyed. 'Who the goddamn hell are *you*?'

'Name's Hannigan. Had me a long talk with your daughter this morning. She told me things about you I reckon will haunt me most of my remaining days.'

Bradly glared, a bit more sober now. 'You got no right here. Get out of my house.'

Hannigan's expression remained grim, unswerving. 'I intend to. But you're coming with me.'

'W-what?'

'Get up. We're going outside. You got any prayer you think will make the journey to Hell an easier trip you best say it now.'

Hannigan gestured with the Peacemaker. Bradly climbed to his feet, weaving. Hannigan urged him out onto the porch then down to the ground. Marcus Bradly saw the noose, then; his eyes widened and a dark stain appeared at the crotch of his trousers.

'What the hell – you can't hang me for lovin' my daughter!'

'Reckon I'd explain the difference between love and rape, Mr Bradly, but I expect it wouldn't matter to you. Get on the horse. . . .'

Bradly hesitated and Hannigan gestured with the gun.

Bradly's entire body trembled now. He blinked,

licked his lips. 'No, this ain't right, she's my daughter. I was just teachin' her how to be a woman.'

'Way I see it, you were ruining her as a woman. With you gone she just might have the chance to be one now.'

Bradly clutched at the saddle horn, hands quaking. He pulled himself up. Terror rode his features as he looked down at Hannigan and the manhunter had to remind himself what the man had done to his daughter, what he truly was, to suppress the measure of guilt and sympathy for another human being that rose within him. But this man wasn't human. He was a sickness, an evil.

'Put the noose around your neck,' Hannigan said.

Panic flashed in Bradly's eyes. 'No, you go to hell! You can't do this. I got a right to a trial!'

Hannigan skritched back the Peacemaker's hammer. 'Do it or I'll just shoot you where you sit.'

Bradly peered down at him, lips stuttering, then looked at the noose. With trembling fingers he gripped the rope, slipped it over his head.

'Tighten it,' Hannigan ordered.

'This ain't fair. This ain't right. Please . . . I love my daughter. She needed me teachin' her how to be a woman. . . .'

'You still don't think you did anything wrong, do you, Bradly?'

'You can't hang me for this. No jury would convict me for takin' care of my girl. I ain't done nothin' wrong.'

Hannigan reached into his pocket, pulled out a wad of folded papers. After stepping up to the horse, he jammed the papers into one of Bradly's trouser pockets.

'Spent some time looking through dodgers. Your dead wife know you were a wanted man before she married you, Mr Bradly? I'm figurin' she didn't. Multiple rapes in Wyoming, the murders of three young women in Texas. List goes on. It's all there in your pocket. Dead or alive, the papers say. I know which way your daughter prefers it.' Hannigan grabbed the horse's reins and drew the big roan from beneath Marcus Bradly. His hazel eyes were hard, resolute, despite the sudden burst of pleading from the killer. It wasn't a pleasant job, but it had to be done.

He waited until Bradly stopped twitching, then went back to town. He didn't bother to cut the man down.

Night seemed softer somehow without the threat of Alejandro del Pelado hanging over them, Jim Hannigan thought, as he gazed across the table at Tootie. They sat at a table in the Regency restaurant, a lavish eatery he wasn't totally comfortable in, but since it was a special night, he'd decided to do it up right. She wore the new dress he'd bought her. Soft blue with frills, it accentuated her sleek curves. He reckoned she was the most beautiful creature he'd ever laid eyes on. For the first time he could recollect, he wore a suit coat, boiled shirt and new trousers. The shirt collar made his neck itch and jitters over what he intended to ask her made his palms damp. He wiped them on the cloth napkin, hoping she didn't notice.

Over the clinking of glasses and the singing of a young woman on the stage, they finished their meal without words. He could tell her thoughts wandered to her brother at times by the dark and infinitely sad look that washed into her mahogany eyes. His death was sinking in, and it would take time for her to come to terms with it.

He sipped his coffee, gathering his courage, and wished to hell he could stop sweating.

She gazed at him, raising an eyebrow. 'You feeling all right?'

'Fine,' he said. 'Just a mite stuffy in here.'

She shrugged. 'Really? Doesn't feel stuffy.' Her gaze dropped to a spot on the table, then returned to him. 'Thank you for the dress. It's beautiful. I always wanted something like this but never had occasion to wear one.'

He cleared his throat, pried at the shirt collar, which felt suddenly choking. 'Thought maybe you could wear it to the wedding. . . .' The words tumbled out before he could stop them and he breathed a sigh of relief. He had been afraid he wouldn't be able to utter a sound.

'Wedding?' A puzzled look crossed her face.

Hand shaking, he drew the box from his coat pocket and slid it across the table.

She opened it and her eyes widened. Her lips began to quiver and a tear slipped from her eye. Light from the chandelier glittered from the ring, painting her cheeks with stars.

'If you'll have me,' he said.

Tootie pulled the ring from the box and slid it onto her finger. She reached across the table and grasped his hand, smiled.

'Reckon I'll have you.'

CHAPTER TEN

Three days later. . . .

The interior of the Methodist church, recently built, glowed with bright rays of noon sunlight that streamed though the stained-glass windows. Jim Hannigan stood on the altar, dressed in his new suit coat and crisply pressed trousers. A string tie adorned his boiled shirt. His neck still itched, but he resisted the urge to fidget. The only aberration was the Peacemaker holstered at his hip. Some habits died hard, and with Hicks and the two hard-cases still on the loose he refused to take any chances.

Beside him stood Tootie. Radiant in her new blue dress, she looked lovely enough to drive a cardinal to sin. Her face beamed, aglow with sunlight; she was an angel and at that moment he was the luckiest man in the world.

'We are gathered here . . .' the minister standing before them began, and butterflies fluttered in his belly. 'To join this man and this woman in the bonds of holy matrimony. . . .'

He shifted his feet, eyes darting nervously to the three young women standing to Tootie's left, the two rescued daughters and Druella Bradly, all of whom wore blue gingham. The young women's fathers stood to his right, Hanly foremost, holding a velvet pillow with the wedding bands he and Tootie had selected from the same shop in which he'd purchased her engagement ring.

'Do you, Angela Maria del Pelado, take this man to be your lawfully wedded husband, to cherish and to hold, in sickness and in health, till death brings you asunder?'

Tootie glazed at him, smiled. 'I do.'

'Do you, James T. Hannigan—'

'I do,' he answered before the minister could go through his speech. He'd never been one for ceremony and his legs were shaking so bad he reckoned if he didn't get this done he was going to make a fool of himself by toppling down the three stairs leading to the aisle.

The minister frowned and Tootie shook her head. Druella Bradly giggled.

The minister resumed. 'If there is anyone here who should object to this union, let him speak now or forever—'

The double doors at the front of the church burst open. The minister swallowed anything further he intended to say and his gaze skipped in that direction. Hannigan whirled, his own gaze following the minister's. A gasp came from Tootie and one of the girls uttered a chopped bleat of terror.

A ghost stood in the doorway, a gun gripped in bleached fingers, aimed towards Jim Hannigan. Face blistered, raw, covered with blackened patches, he looked like a figure from a nightmare. Much of his long dark hair had burned away to stringy patches falling from a scabbed pate. His clothes were soot-covered, torn. The look in his one exposed eye was that of a rabid animal, vicious, enraged, insane. He lumbered forward, steps dragging.

'Alejandro. . . .' Tootie whispered, her face suddenly pale, her body trembling. Hannigan stepped in front of her, shielding her body with his own in case Alejandro shifted his aim to her.

'I object to this union, Hannigan,' said Alejandro. 'I object most powerfully.' He laughed, a sound pregnant with madness. His gaze swept across the others present, then returned to the manhunter.

'This isn't the place, del Pelado.' Hannigan came down a step.

Alejandro's expression didn't change. 'Isn't it? This is a holy place, is it not? An arena for birth and death . . . for resurrection. You see, Mr Hannigan, you can't kill me. I'm a god now. I've been reborn. I've been given this chance to finish what I should have finished in Angel Pass. I have been resurrected to kill you.'

'Leave us be, Alejandro.' Tootie stepped out from behind Hannigan. Sadness mixed with anger darkened her face.

Alejandro's gaze leveled on her, cold, lacking any semblance of brotherly love. 'Dear sister, I gave you every chance to join me, but you refused. While I cannot understand that, I accept it. But I will not allow you to marry him. I'd sooner see you dead.'

Tears glossed Tootie's eyes, but didn't flow. 'Please, Alejandro . . . don't do this. As your sister I'm begging you. . . .'

He laughed again, a vicious sound. 'As I recall, you disavowed any relationship to me six months ago. You left me to die on the gallows.'

It was coming. Hannigan saw it. Alejandro was going to pull the trigger. The only doubt that remained was whom would he fire at first – him or Tootie?

A sound came from the front doors. A jar hurtled into the church and smashed against the floor. With a *whoosh*, flames burst out. Fire streaked in line across the threshold.

Alejandro had not come alone.

'I've decided we should all die this time,' Alejandro said. 'I won't let any of you leave. It's only fitting, don't you think?'

'You're mad,' Tootie said.

He smiled. 'Quite. Perhaps I have been since the day James Deadwood destroyed our childhood.'

One of the girls screamed. She had lost her nerve at the sight of the flames.

Alejandro del Pelado started at the sound, jerked his gun towards the shrieking young woman.

Tootie doubled, grabbed the bottom of her dress and lifted. Beneath, strapped to her thigh, was her derringer, which Hannigan had retrieved from the marshal's office. She seized it, brought it to aim on her brother.

At the same time, Hannigan launched himself at the former circus man. Alejandro tried to swing his gun back to the manhunter, but didn't make it in time. Tootie withheld fire: Hannigan's body was now shielding her brother's.

He crashed into Alejandro, knocked the outlaw from his feet. Hannigan came down atop him, but the circus man somehow managed to retain his hold on the gun and get an arm free. He clubbed at Hannigan's head with its butt. The weapon clacked from his temple in a glancing blow and stars burst before his eyes.

Stunned, acting on instinct, Hannigan jammed a forearm into Alejandro's throat and thrust. Alejandro made gagging sounds; his face washed purple.

Hannigan, sight returning, sent a chopping blow into the man's face, but at the poor angle, with them rolling on the floor, it carried little power.

It bought him a moment's respite, however. He tore himself from Alejandro's grip and rolled back. Quickly rising to his feet, he doubled, grabbed two handfuls of Alejandro's shirt and hauled him up. Alejandro swung the gun at Hannigan's face; Hannigan jerked his head sideways and the weapon sailed over his shoulder.

Releasing Alejandro, the manhunter arced an uppercut that clacked the killer's teeth together and snapped his head backward. Even stunned, he held onto the gun, fingers white in a death-grip.

Alejandro staggered, on the verge of collapse. Hannigan stepped in, ready to finish it.

A sudden insane light blazed in the circus man's eyes. He whipped up the gun, pressed it against Hannigan's chest. The move caught the manhunter by surprise; he had thought Alejandro out on his feet, but rage and insanity had infused the man with almost superhuman stamina.

A malicious smile waxed over Alejandro's lips. He was an instant away from pulling the trigger.

A shot came, an exaggerated pop that reverberated from the church walls. Hannigan jerked to the left, but the move proved unnecessary.

Alejandro del Pelado froze. Any sense of victory vanished from his eye.

The outlaw turned, his movements jerky, uncoordinated. His one-eyed gaze focused on Tootie, who stood at the bottom of the altar, the derringer held straight-armed before her. Tears ran down her face, dripped onto her dress.

'Angela . . .' Alejandro's voice came in a gurgle, weak. 'How . . . how could you?'

A sob racked her body. Her hands shook on the derringer. 'You gave me no choice, Alejandro. I couldn't let you hurt him. I couldn't let you hurt anyone ever again. . . .'

He laughed a fluid laugh. 'Maybe I was wrong . . . maybe you are strong – after all. . . .'

'No!' yelled Hannigan, making a move toward Alejandro. He saw the circus man's gun hand jerk up and around.

Alejandro leveled the gun on Tootie before he

150

even stopped speaking. As his final act, he intended
to take his sister with him.

Tootie was ready for it. She pulled the derringer's
trigger. The second bullet punched into Alejandro's
chest, kicking him back a step. His gun hand
wavered; the Smith & Wesson slipped from his grip,
dropped to the floor. He looked down at his chest.
His hands came up, pressed against the wound as if
he were trying to stanch the blood pumping from a
hole above his heart.

He looked up at her with an almost childlike
expression. A thin smile drifted onto his lips. 'Thank
you . . .' he whispered, then collapsed to his knees.
'Angela . . . be . . . be . . . strong. . . .'

Alejandro fell face forward, slammed into the
floor, then went still.

Sobs racked Tootie as she ran to him. She dropped
beside her brother and pulled his head to her breast.
Blood washed onto her dress and tears streamed
from her eyes.

Something in Hannigan's belly plunged, but he
had no time to dwell on the tragedy before him. His
gaze lifted to the front. Flame skittered across the
floor and along the wall to the sides of both doors.

Shots suddenly blasted from beyond one door.
Bullets plowed through stained-glass windows, shat-
tering them. Variegated slivers of glass twirled to the
floor.

'There's blankets in the back room!' the minister
yelled to the girls and the two fathers, who stood
frozen, aghast at what had just occurred.

'Go!' Hannigan yelled. He whipped his

151

Peacemaker from its holster, then ran down the aisle. He would have preferred seeing to Tootie but at least one man was outside, firing in on them.

The fathers bolted into the back room, a moment later returning with bundles of woolen blankets. They handed them to the girls, except for Druella, who refused. The young woman ran down the short steps to the aisle and grabbed Alejandro's Smith & Wesson, then darted towards the back.

As the two men and their daughters slapped blankets at the flames great clouds of smoke billowed up. Hannigan used the smoke to his advantage, as cover to peer out at the church's front grounds. Eyes stinging, he spotted a man, standing about twenty feet away, behind a cottonwood: Hicks. The marshal had exposed part of himself, preparatory to taking a shot. Hannigan fired.

A yelp came from the marshal as the bullet tore across his shoulder. He jumped back. Hannigan leaped through the doorway.

Seeing a boulder ten feet to the right, he hurtled down the stairs to the ground. Triggering shots towards the lawdog, he reached the boulder, got behind it. Lead spanged at his heels from two other locations and he knew the marshal had back-up, likely the two Nancy hardcases. He smiled a grim smile, pegged one who was hiding behind a wagon and the other, who was a hundred feet to the left, crouched behind a marble gate-column.

He hunkered down, reloaded with bullets tucked in his belt, then peered out.

The marshal instantly fired. Stone chipped from

the boulder, stinging his face. He returned fire. Lead splintered tree wood but did no damage to the lawdog.

'Give it up, Hannigan!' the marshal yelled. 'There's no way out.'

'Alejandro's dead, Hicks!' Hannigan yelled back. 'You got no leader. Give yourself up and maybe you won't hang.'

A laugh gave him his answer.

Two more shots came in unison, fired at the sound of his voice by the two hardcases. He tried to draw a bead on the one behind the wagon, fired, but missed.

They were at a stalemate. No one was going anywhere till somebody ran out of bullets or the church burned down.

A shot broke his reverie. Followed by a second. Neither bullet hit close to him and he wondered what the hell was going on. He edged up, peered toward the marshal's position. The lawman lay on the ground, unmoving. Druella Bradly stood ten feet to Hannigan's left. She had gone out by a back way and circled behind the marshal. He must have spotted her and fired a hasty shot because his body was half-twisted on the ground. Pale, she shook a little as she looked toward Hannigan, frozen by what she had done.

'Get down, Druella!' he yelled.

It was too late. One of the hardcases had leaped up from behind the wagon and was drawing a bead on her.

Hannigan jumped out from behind the boulder,

fired, hoping merely to draw the man's aim so the young woman could reach cover.

The little hardcase never shifted aim. He was intent on killing the girl. He would have, too, but Druella, startled into action, pulled the trigger again. The man jolted, a blossom of crimson appearing on his chest. He crumpled to the ground, gun dropping from his grip.

A shriek came, and the second hardcase suddenly bolted from behind the marble column and ran to his fallen partner.

'You goddamn savages!' he yelled, sinking beside the wounded man, then pulling him to his breast. 'You killed him! You killed him!'

'What the hell?' Hannigan muttered. He glanced at Druella, unsure whether the girl was going to shoot the second man just for all the wailing he was doing.

He went to the young woman, whose arms shook as she straight-armed the Smith & Wesson.

Hannigan took the gun from her, shoved it in his belt. 'I owe you a debt, Druella,' he said.

She gazed at him, the stain of death naked in her eyes. 'No, Mr Hannigan, I owed you. Not sure I'll ever be able to repay you and Tootie for all you've done, but I figure helpin' against those bastards was the least I could do.'

Hannigan guided the young woman back to the church steps and holstered his own gun. She sat on the stone and buried her face in her hands. He heard her sobbing as he walked towards the still shrieking hardcase. He reckoned she was going to have a time dealing with the fact she'd taken two lives, even if it was to save her friends.

Hannigan stopped near the hardcases, peering down. The one named Mr Rory peered up, tears flowing from his eyes.

'I loved him, you sonofabitch.' He spat at Hannigan's shoe.

'You had a damn peculiar way of showing it, I figure.'

'You don't know what it was like. . . .'

Hannigan shook his head, frowned. 'No, I don't. Can't confess to understandin' your type, but I reckon if you two hadn't gone about your lives trying to hurt others you might have been a hell of a lot happier and your friend might still be alive. Where's your gun?'

Mr Rory nudged his head over towards the marble column. Hannigan knelt and picked up Mr Ryan's piece.

'Get up. You're going in the church till I can get you to a cell.'

'What about him?' Mr Rory ducked his chin at Mr Ryan.

Hannigan was tempted to say let the buzzards have him. 'I'll see to it he's buried. That's more than either of you deserves.'

Mr Rory nodded, then gently placed his partner's head on the ground. He stood. Hannigan began to turn to go back to the church, first gesturing with the Smith & Wesson that belonged to the deceased hardcase.

'Mr Hannigan. . . .' said Mr Rory and the

manhunter froze. Mr Rory had slipped another gun, a derringer, from his pocket, and Hannigan felt like a fool for not being more careful.

Mr Rory looked at him, more pain washing into his eyes than Hannigan had ever witnessed in a man. 'I can't live without him. . . .' Mr Rory swept the derringer to his temple and fired. His head jerked and his eyes went dull. He staggered, fell over backwards.

Hannigan's mouth came open. 'I'll be damned. . . .' he whispered.

He returned to the church, walked up the stairs past the girl, who still sobbed into her hands. Inside, the two other young women and their fathers had managed to smother the fire. Black smoke whirled in the air and much of the floor and wall about the doorway was charred. The minister was bending over Tootie. Hannigan set the Smith & Wesson on a pew and went to her. The minister gave him a pained look then moved away.

'Tootie. . . .' he whispered, reaching out a hand.

She looked up, tears on her face, sadness in her eyes. 'I was just recollecting the time when we were young'uns. He protected me, stopped others from hurting me.'

'I reckon in the last minute he knew you returned the favor, Tootie. He was mad; he would have gone on killing and hurting ohers. He couldn't stop himself. You had no choice and you saved my life.'

She nodded, lower lip quivering. 'I know . . . I just wish . . . things would have somehow turned out different. . . .'

She set Alejandro's head on the floor and came to her feet. Blood had ruined the front of her new dress.

Hannigan took her in his arms. She sobbed as he led her from the church.

EPILOG

Two weeks later. . . .

Some of the restoration to the church floor and walls had been finished but there was still work to be completed. The minister had agreed to redo the ceremony but made Jim Hannigan promise no more killers would show up on the doorstep to interrupt the proceedings.

They stood where they had stood three weeks ago, he and Tootie at the altar, Druella, the two young women and their fathers to either side. Druella had recovered fine, in his estimation. She was a strong young lady.

'If we may begin. . . .' the minister said.

Hannigan had bought Tootie a new dress, a traditional white gown with lace. He wore the same jacket and string tie, and a new shirt.

'We can skip the front part and just get right to it,' Hannigan said, with a slight grin.

'The hell we can!' Tootie said, her smile wider than his. Then, 'Forgive me, Pastor.'

The minister nodded, lips pursed. 'That's quite all

right, Miss del Pelado.'

Tootie turned to Hannigan. 'I went through hell to get to this point, I want the whole package.'

He grinned, took her hand in his.

'We are gathered here today to join this man and this woman. . . .' the minister began.

This time there were no interruptions. Hannigan reckoned the events that had occurred three weeks ago would fade only with time, but the vows he spoke to her today would carry on forever. As he placed the band on her finger he knew that for at least one time in his life fate was smiling on him.